Vigil For A Stranger

Vigil For A Stranger

KITTY BURNS FLOREY

Broken Moon Press · Seattle

The characters and events in this novel are fictitious. Any similarity between them and real persons, living or dead, or events is coincidental.

Cover image, "St. Georges Island, Maine," by Elizabeth Hope Shaw. Used by permission. Author photo © 1994 by Juliana Spear. Used by permission. Excerpt from "All I Have To Do Is Dream," words and music by Boudleaux Bryant. © 1958 Boudleaux Bryant. House of Bryant Publications. All rights reserved. Used by permission.

Printed in the United States of America.

ISBN 0-913089-43-5

Project editor: Lesley Link
Copy editor/proofreader: Paula Ladenburg
Text preparation by: Melissa Shaw

Broken Moon Press
Post Office Box 24585
Seattle, Washington 98124-0585 USA

For Turi MacCombie

PART ONE

Dream

Whenever I want you, all I have to do is dream.

The Everly Brothers

Chapter One

I had just been thinking about Pierce when I saw his name.

That I was thinking of him was not unusual. Twenty years had gone by, and still he was in my mind nearly every day—sometimes for a moment, other times like an extended meditation. For one thing, I still had so many objects associated with him. The wind-up penguin (though the mechanism was stuck, and the penguin would no longer waddle off the tabletop on its webbed orange feet). A paperback volume of Van Gogh's letters to his brother. The picnic basket (in which I kept needlepoint yarn). A snapshot of Pierce and me in front of his apartment house on Orange Street. Plus a lot of little, lesser stuff—a postcard of "The Night Café," a book of matches from Tynan's (now defunct), a couple of playbills, an empty box that used to contain Marlboros (mine) and now contained dozens of those tiny seashells like thumbnails that we picked up at Plover Island.

But I would have thought of him even without these literal reminders. The world—life—myself: everything recalled Pierce to me, there was no help for it, no escaping now any more than twenty years ago. I didn't even want to escape: thinking of Pierce, remembering him, hadn't been painful for a long time.

I was on the 9:02 train to New York. At Bridgeport, the punk Yalie sitting next to me got off, and a woman in a business suit got on—briefcase in one hand, tidy overnight bag in the other. She paused briefly in the aisle, with that impersonally hostile look a certain kind of professional woman tends to cultivate—the look that says: don't you dare mess with me because I'm not only busy, I'm *special*. Calculating the seating possibilities, she settled for me, probably only because I had a book in front of me and looked harmless, but I was flattered—the way her suit might have felt when she chose it over a dozen others that were similar but not quite, quite right.

She swung her bag onto the rack over my head and sat down without a further glance at me, her briefcase in her lap and her hands folded on it. She leaned back in her seat with a private little sigh, and without actually turning to look at her, I imagined her closing her eyes, exhausted by the rigors of Bridgeport, of the presentation she'd had to give, or the fat new account she was trying to nab, the case she was prepared to win, the tension of the upcoming power lunch with a big shot. Whatever it is that wears that kind of person out no matter how much coffee they drink or how many hours they put in at the gym.

Pierce and I used to go on like that: *that kind of person,* we used to say, categorizing, analyzing, coming up with half-baked theories to explain the world, until Charlie would say, "Don't you know there's no truth in generalizing?" and Pierce would reply, "There are two kinds of people in this world, Charlie—the ones who believe in generalizations, and the ones who don't."

The train lurched out of the Bridgeport station and south along the back ends of warehouses brightened with graffiti. Thinking idly of Pierce and those dear, dead days—not with sorrow, but with a simple pleasure in knowing that he, they, had once existed—I studied my seatmate out of the corner of my eye. Grey wool suit, slightly flared skirt discreetly below the knee but not so far below that it looked *à la Bohème* (as mine, nearly ankle-length, surely did). Silky cream-colored blouse, whose pearl-buttoned cuffs I could just glimpse below the grey sleeves. High-tech watch on the left wrist, thin gold bangle on the right, no rings, no nail polish except possibly one coat of clear (hard to tell). Sheer, shiny stockings, good black shoes with sensible heels. Wine-colored expanding briefcase with black saddle-stitching around a pair of shaped, flat handles. Age, deduced from backs of hands (wiry—the kind that with time would become simian—but, so far, relatively unlined), about thirty-four.

I was about to return to my book when she stirred in her seat and sighed a different kind of sigh—determined, dutiful, a touch grim (though still private, not the kind of ostentatious sigh designed to elicit conversation)—and opened the briefcase. I imagined her saying to herself as she boarded the train: three minutes to flop, baby, and then it's back to work for you, you don't get ahead by napping on trains. The first thing she did was to pull out a bulging black leather Filo-Fax. Of course. Even Charlie would have to see the Filo-Fax, with its neatly tabbed compartments for datebook, addresses, expense-account records, personal diary, you-name-it, as irrefutable proof that she was a type, a screaming generalization. "You know, Pierce—a yuppie," Charlie would say in his patient, hesitating way. Except that yuppies hadn't been invented when Pierce died, and perhaps Filo-Faxes hadn't, either. In my mind, I saw Pierce's inquiring face, his head tipped sideways, his ironic, excessively helpless smile: "Yuppie, Charles?" Forget it, Pierce, I thought. It's too hard to explain—as if he were a character in one of those books or films where someone in history is flung into the twentieth century, or vice versa. Shakespeare turning up in a fast food place in California, or a little urban kid being transported back to pioneer times. *See, this is a Big Mac, Will. This is what we call a Conestoga wagon, Tiffany.*

The woman crossed her legs, swinging one foot out into the aisle and bouncing it up and down (irritably, as an extension of her hostile, off-putting look), and flipped open the Filo-Fax to her appointments for that week, bending her head over her little book so that her long-ish (but not too long), blondish (ditto) hair obscured the page. I spent an idle moment envying her hair, which was really quite beautiful—thick, straight, and artfully streaked—and then I lost interest and returned to *Swann's Way*.

I had read *Swann's Way* a million times—or a dozen, or six, I don't know. I'd read it a lot. I never progressed to the rest of Proust. *Swann's Way* was enough for me—the book that had everything, as far as I was concerned—my own personal Filo-Fax. My French ex-husband, Emile, gave it to me, the old Scott Moncrieff translation, for my birthday—my first birthday with him, when we were still pretty happy—and said he'd give me a volume every year. One volume a year of *Remembrance of Things Past* was enough, he said—even in

English. Enough for you, anyway, was what he implied. I think he expected me to spend the whole year reading it, if I read it at all. Emile never had much respect for my intelligence, still less for my diligence, but the day after that birthday (my twenty-sixth) I came down with a mild case of flu—just enough to send me to bed and get Emile to wait on me in a low-key sort of way (tea when I called for it, a little canned broth, he even went out for ginger ale)—and wolfed down *Swann's Way* in three feverish days. Then I read it again when I was well, and again when we went to Vermont for a week's vacation. I think Emile was torn between a sort of shocked pride in me and disappointment: he too liked his generalizations, and the fact that he'd read Proust and I hadn't gave him a superiority over me that he wasn't crazy about relinquishing.

He continued to give me a volume a year. Emile was like that: organized, methodical, French, and when he said he was going to do something he did it. The Proust piled up, even though I never did read another volume. Denis was born, and I didn't have much time or energy for reading. And soon after the seventh and last volume appeared, I had my breakdown and Emile went back to France, taking Denis, leaving me the Proust, complete—a sort of souvenir, I suppose. As a way of punishing him, I included those last six volumes in a bunch of stuff I gave to a tag sale that benefited Denis's old nursery school. Not much of a punishment—not a punishment that fit the crime—and certainly not an even trade: a five-year-old boy for six volumes of Proust donated to charity. Emile never knew what happened to the books, anyway (or to me, not that he cared) since we didn't communicate for nearly a year. But getting those books off my back (they were exquisite, small, tiny-printed hardcover things, I think he ordered them from someplace in England) gave me a certain kind of happiness at a time when very little happiness was available to me.

It wasn't Emile I thought about when I opened the book, though: it was Pierce. Or actually, of course, it was little Marcel. I was at the point where, after Marcel's mother has finally come into his room to read him to sleep (*François le Champi* without the love scenes), he gives us his thoughts on the difficulties of recapturing the past, and then on to the tea and the famous madeleine and the passage about the

Celtic belief that the souls of the dead are imprisoned in trees or plants or objects, and then of course I thought of Pierce, as I always did when I read those words. How after he died—before I'd even read Proust or heard this particular Celtic belief—I used to find him again in trees, how it seemed he was with me if I stood with my back pressed to the trunk of a tree, or my cheek against the bark. Specifically, I sought this feeling—this Pierce-ness, this sense of being filled with a sort of essence of Pierce, of being "pierced"—from one particular grove of trees that grew behind my parents' place, between the house and the pond. All that summer, when I was back home trying to get a grip on things, trying to assimilate his being gone (I would come to terms with it some other time, that summer I was having trouble just believing it), all that summer, I sat out in the yard at the edge of that grove of young birches and a couple of more substantial maples—and I couldn't stop believing that Pierce (or a certain Pierce-ness) was there with me. Which was partly why I was having trouble accepting things, the sensation was so strong.

This is what I was remembering when I looked up from that passage and happened to glance over at the Filo-Fax, now visible on my seatmate's lap, spread out forgotten on her briefcase, still opened to the week of October 24, while she read a bluecovered folder held close to her eyes (maybe her glasses were in the overnight bag). I wondered what it would be like to have a life so complicated it needed a Filo-Fax to organize it. The concept didn't sound appealing to me. Every day was crammed with entries except for the day before (Monday, the 24th), which was at the top of the page and said simply, "Casco Industries, Bridgeport." She'd gone up to Bridgeport, then, with her presentation or sales pitch or takeover bid, she'd stayed late impressing her fellow executives at dinner and after, spent the night in some hideous Hilton or Sheraton, and was on the way back to Manhattan. To the home office of the corporation that employed her? Or perhaps she traveled all over, presenting or pitching or gobbling up new accounts or whatever she did in a suit like that, in those shoes.

Idly, I speculated about her private life (she'd gone to Princeton, she played racquetball, she was involved with a banker named Jeff, and did she ever sleep with the various corporate managers etc. that she met with on these trips?), eyeing her engagements for that week in October—gym date with someone, gym date with someone else (I imagined brutal racquetball games, then cold white wine in the sauna), lunch with someone, dinner w/R (three times—O.K., so his name wasn't Jeff but Randy), a meeting with J.D.N.—and it took me a moment to understand what I was seeing: on Thursday the 27th, I read, "Orin Pierce, 1:30, Chez D."

No. It couldn't say that, of course. How funny, though: it looked like Orin Pierce. I tried to focus on it, leaning slightly too intimately close to her (blinkered by her blue folder, she didn't seem to notice). Owen Price? Olive Pounce? Her handwriting was messy (*I'm so busy*) but artistic (*I'm so special*). The 1:30 was clear. Chez D. could have been Chez O. or Chez C. But Orin Pierce. It did seem to say Orin Pierce. No. It couldn't possibly. Of course, the world could be full of Orin Pierces. But it was an unusual name, surely. I remembered how much Pierce hated Orin, and refused to answer to it. I rather liked Orin: an out of fashion, vaguely agricultural-sounding name (though Pierce grew up outside New Haven, the son of Yale professors), but distinctive, a name that could plausibly belong to someone famous— senator, novelist, historian. Pierce was an actor, so it was perfect. Orin Pierce. I bent over to do something to my shoe, and brought my face on a level with the yuppie's lap: Orin Pierce? The Pierce was clear enough, Orin could have been Owen—no, there was definitely a dot, there had to be an i. Olin? Wasn't there a corporation called Olin? Maybe it wasn't a person at all, maybe it was another presentation, another pitch. Olin, Orwell, Olwin, Orin, Orin, Orin Pierce.

She snapped the Filo-Fax shut and returned it to her briefcase with the blue folder. I leaned back in my seat, my face toward the window, and realized I was shaking, sweating, there were tears in my eyes. I clutched my book with both hands, brought it to my chest, hugged it. Reflected in the window I could see the pale blob of my face, and, outside, an abandoned factory, the back of a shopping center, a Syrian luncheonette, a coin shop, a gas station . . .

Pierce, I thought. *Pierce.* I had to force myself not to cry out.

And then I thought: ask her. *Excuse me, I couldn't help but notice in your datebook, there was the name of someone I used to know, I wasn't being nosy, really, it just happened to catch my eye, someone I used to know, who died a long time ago, twenty years ago last June, and I wondered if you could tell me*—The woman stood up just then, laid her briefcase down on the seat, and reached for her bag. The crackling loudspeaker said, "Stamford station, next stop. Stamford next. Watch your step, please."

I was seized with panic. I looked up at her. She was struggling with her bag, which was wedged under something else. When she reached her arms up, her blouse had come loose from her skirt; an inch of smooth white slip was showing above the waistband. I glanced down at the briefcase. I hadn't noticed before the tag attached to it—same leather, plastic-covered, with a business card slipped inside: Alison Kaye, it said. Haver & Schmidt. The rest was in classy upper-case lettering too tiny to read, though I tried, bending down to my shoe again, leaning toward the tag until I was nearly on top of it.

As if she were determined to thwart me, she snatched up the briefcase, her bag recovered, and stepped out into the aisle behind a man in a bomber jacket, moving toward the front of the car: grey back, very straight, a bag dangling from each hand, blondish hair parting around her collar as she bent her head, then turn and down the steps: gone. While I sat there trembling.

I would have followed her off the train, into the Stamford station, out to her taxi or the waiting corporate limo or across the street to one of those gleaming office buildings Stamford is famous for, if there had been more time—or less time, because I think that what finally stopped me wasn't just a failure to act quickly but a memory of twelve years ago, when I had my breakdown, when I thought I'd seen Robbie, thought he'd visited me, we'd had tea together, and cookies, and—what else? I've forgotten some of the details of that vision now. It was absurd, of course. I was suffering from the trip to Plover Island and from Emile's coldness, all that had made me peculiar, made me see things, imagine things, my brother drinking tea with me, talking.

Twelve years ago I ended up in the hospital: Yale–New Haven, where I learned to make baskets. And there was no Robbie, of course, just as there was no Pierce. It can take a long time for that kind of shock to leave the system, my shrink said, holding my hand. Old Dr. Dalziel, whose hair had turned white (I was told by a nurse) during the six months it took his wife to die of cancer. "Those were terrible things that happened to you, Christine," he said. "It's certainly not unusual that they affected you strongly, that you haven't been able to accept them, you're still grieving." His white hair was brushed back from his high pink forehead, and his hand that held mine was curled from arthritis. He said: "You're not crazy, please stop saying that right now."

Owen Price. Olive Prince.

I let my book fall into the lap. I lay back and closed my eyes, as my seatmate had when she first got on the train. Owen Price, Olive Prince. I breathed deeply, and calmed down. Stamford, yes. Then Greenwich. Then express to 125th Street, then Grand Central. Get on an uptown bus. Go to the Frick, meet Silvie at 1:00. Lunch. Talk. George Drescher at the Aurora Gallery 4:00. Then maybe a drink at the Oyster Bar and home on the 6:22, the 6:47 at the latest. Train, James, home, a bite of something good, and bed. Bed, and then it would be tomorrow, and things always look different tomorrow. Tell James about this? Maybe—so that he can grip my wrists and say, *He's dead, Christine. You know he is. He's dead, don't do this to yourself*—the way Charlie did twenty years ago, yelling at me when I refused to believe it. *Pierce is dead, Chris—dead dead dead.*

I did calm down. I did begin to breathe regularly, the sweat dried on my back, I even returned to my book: Marcel and the madeleine and the tea—the scene, I figured out years ago with my shrink, that had probably been the inspiration for my own mad vision of Robbie coming to drink tea with me and take me into the past. I read, with pleasure and absorption and the love I always felt for the rich complex sentences, the elaborate and beautiful comparisons, the wistful remembering—but the business card stayed in my mind, crisp black letters on white: Alison Kaye, Haver & Schmidt.

And I kept hearing Pierce's voice in my head: "There are two kinds of people in this world, Charles—people who get over things and people who don't."

~

Pierce was killed when his car went off a cliff in New Mexico. The car plunged 300 feet, straight down. The bodies were smashed beyond recognition—or almost. They were eventually found, retrieved, identified—teeth, whatever. I never got the details. The car, at any rate, was Pierce's old VW, the one he had driven out there—the ancient rattletrap he'd owned for as long as I'd known him. There were two people with him, a man and a woman, no one I'd ever heard of. Think of that death, the spin into air, the going down. How long would it take? What would his last words be? "Holy shit" or "Help" or "Jesus Christ" or "No!" Or a wild "Whoopee" of delight.

Charlie broke it to me. I was living in a town in eastern Pennsylvania, north of Philadelphia—not far from Charlie's home town, in fact. I had a job as an office temporary in an insurance firm where I stood all day in a huge, over-airconditioned room filing pink forms in tan folders in blue filing cabinets. My arms ached, my feet hurt. I had never hated a job so much, but the pay wasn't bad, and I liked the shabby little town.

Charlie was still in New Haven, living in the Orange Street apartment he had shared with Pierce, doing what I don't remember—working at Sterling Library, I think. He drove all the way down to tell me in person. He'd seen it on television—a tragedy so spectacular it might have made the news even if Pierce hadn't been a local boy. Charlie knew I didn't have a television. He showed up at my apartment—an odd little place in the back of an old gabled house, up a flight of rickety outside steps. He stood at my kitchen door, looking at me through the screen. I hadn't heard him approach: I had my noisy fan on, it was a hot night. He said, "Christine," and I looked up and ran to let him in.

I hadn't seen him in months. He cried in my arms for a long time before he could tell me. I kept saying, "Charlie, what is it, what is it?"—terrified. I was afraid, for some reason, that he had done something awful—murdered someone, been involved in a hit-and-run. I have no idea why I thought that. Charlie was a model citizen, he was sober, he was serious, he was controlled—that was his self, and that was also his curious, reassuring charm (that and his Huck Finn looks). He was a relentlessly good person, who had never done a mean or violent or even thoughtless thing in his life—maybe that was why my first thought was that he finally had. Seeing him cry was so horrible that it seemed anything could have happened—as if a building that's stood for centuries (Chartres, Windsor Castle) should suddenly crumble, and collapse with a sigh that sounded human.

Finally, of course, he stopped crying. He blew his nose, went to the sink, washed his face and dried it on a dishtowel. I gave him a beer. He said, "Maybe you'd better have one too," and then he sat down across the kitchen table and said, "Pierce is dead. I heard it on the news."

~

Charlie and Pierce and I became friends in college. We were all from small towns—Pierce from a shoreline town in Connecticut, Charlie from eastern Pennsylvania, me from upstate New York. That was our bond at Oberlin, a small-town school where everyone else seemed to be from Manhattan or Chicago. Most of the other people we knew were going quietly crazy in Oberlin, Ohio, a dry town with a two-block main drag. There were a lot of desperate trips to Cleveland, all-night drives to Chicago, a lot of transferring out. Charlie and Pierce and I were perfectly content with the town, with our lives—most of the time with each other. The three of us were inseparable, especially during our last two years when so many of our friends had left.

Technically, I suppose I was Charlie's girlfriend, but Pierce and I were best friends, together more than Charlie and I were, or Pierce and anybody else, any of his dozens of girls. And though we both loved Charlie—oh God, I did love him, Charlie and his red curls, his long legs, his sweet mouth—the truth was that we often considered him a third wheel. He didn't get our jokes, he was always deadly earnest, and he used to suffer intensely when Pierce put on the old blues records he and I were both crazy about.

The only kind of music Charlie could stand was the rock and roll of his high school days, especially anything by the Everly Brothers. *Neat music,* he called it, and meant it literally: Pierce's heroes (Big Bill Broonzy, Little Brother Montgomery, Otis Spann, Sonny Terry and Brownie McGee) represented *messy music,* rambling and guttural, raucous, mumbling, full of extempore piano runs and guitars pushed to their breaking point with bottlenecks and tricky fingering, full of sex and booze and bad trouble. Charlie found the easy harmonies, the polished voices, the tidy a-a-b-a form of the Everly Brothers' songs soothing, and the point of music was to soothe, he said. We could never talk him out of it.

One of his great joys was to harmonize Everly Brothers songs with Pierce—something the two of them used to do on those nights when we were all sitting around Pierce's room (Pierce always managed to get himself a single) and Pierce was getting fed up with Charlie. Pierce's way of coping with occasions like that, when someone bugged him, was to come up with a way out of it that included the person: he'd reach out to, say, Charlie, and draw him in instead of trying to get rid of him. I admired that in Pierce, and when I sensed the tension building up with Charlie, I learned to wait peacefully, suppressing my own irritation with Charlie's stodgy thick-headedness and babyish insistence on his own way, knowing that Pierce would smooth things out, that in a short time all would be well again with the three of us. It was at times like those that Pierce and Charlie would sing. "Bye Bye Love," "Dream," "Devoted to You," and "I Wonder If I Care as Much"—they did them all, but those were their best numbers, the straightforward love songs. They had a gimmick. They were both very musical, with a real gift for close harmony, and what one of them would do, after they had sung straight for a while, was suddenly switch parts, tenor to baritone (Don to Phil), and the other would have to do the same without losing the harmony and without missing a note. They would do this endlessly, switching sometimes in the course of one phrase—Charlie's lighter, slightly tinny but very pleasant voice (he took lessons at the Conservatory on the side, and sang with the Gilbert & Sullivan Society) barging in on Pierce's rougher, deeper one—so that there would be a hiccupy quality to their singing, a strangely looping sound, as if someone were fooling around with the treble/bass switches on a stereo. I used to wait nervously for them to slip up, for a failure of attention or a lapse of technique from either of them—as if I were witnessing some complicated maneuver on which our lives depended. But once they got the hang of it, they were unable to throw each other off, and though sometimes when they sang their voices were wobbly with suppressed laughter, though they glared at each other across the room or gave each other the finger when a particularly difficult challenge had been met, neither of them, over the years, ever failed, that I recall.

~

Charlie was on the West Coast, working for the Los Angeles branch of a big New York literary agency. When I got off the train that day at Grand Central, I was tempted to call his agency on the off-chance that he was in New York. I felt that I needed to talk to someone about my experience on the train—my non-experience, my moment of crazy hope followed by a desolation that was like Pierce dying all over again.

But I did nothing. I had learned ways over the years to protect myself from looking foolish. And I didn't really want to see Charlie. He had become bitter in middle age, the old earnest seriousness turned to high anxiety. His life had gone off the rails over and over; it was like one of the blues records he hated: trouble with women, trouble with jobs, trouble with money. And in his thirties he'd developed chronic asthma that laid him low, it seemed, every time he especially needed to be up for something.

There was a period when he called me a lot, when for several months both of us spent a lot of money we didn't have on coast-to-coast phone calls that were designed mainly to see him through a rough time (he was trying to pay child support out of his unemployment checks) but that also worked the other way (this was not long after Emile left me), and I was still troubled by some of the confessions I had made to him. He talked a lot about our getting together when he was in New York, but we never did. Neither of us really, really wanted to make the doomed effort to reactivate what was once between us—not only the good old friendship (which would be pathetic, parodic, without Pierce) but the good old lust—the simple, supremely rational pleasure in each other's bodies that had, in its way, consoled us for our failure, joint and individual, to fully possess Pierce—a desire, I realized after Pierce died, that was at the heart of our triangular friendship. I think Charlie realized this, too, at last, and that it embarrassed him, it made him awkward with me, it may even have been what embittered him and made his life so difficult, it may even have brought on his asthma.

I hadn't seen him in years, and as I walked up Lexington Avenue I knew I didn't want to see him then, either, and certainly, when I thought about it, I didn't want to tell him about the woman on the train. I imagined him turning away in disgust, in sorrow, in anger—

impossible to predict the exact nature of his reaction, only that it would be negative. I knew he would tell me I needed help, he'd load me down with jargon, with praise for his new doctor and his new medication, and would insist on recommending some New York psychotherapist or other. Charlie always thought therapy would solve everything, even though after years of seeing people on both coasts he was, in my opinion, more screwed-up than ever.

So I walked down 43rd and over to Madison to catch a bus uptown. As always in New York, I felt that disconcerting but far from unpleasant blend of excitement and apprehension: anything could happen here, good or bad. I had once been mugged on Sixth Avenue, around the corner from the Museum of Modern Art, at dusk—my purse ripped from my shoulder, a knife coming out of nowhere to slit the skin of my arm along its length like the peel of a banana—and had had the odd, uniquely big-town experience of helplessness when passers-by recoiled from me instead of coming to my assistance.

On the other hand, at a hot-dog stand near Rockefeller Center, I once ran into Nancy Doyle, a childhood friend who had moved to Texas—someone I had never thought to see again anywhere, and there she was, looking like her fifth-grade self only bigger and better dressed, reaching into her bag for change, then glancing up to see me and breaking into a laugh of amazed delight that matched my own.

And then once, in front of a boutique called La Vie En Rose, an elderly man had come running up to me and screamed—a shrill, soprano screech one would not have thought possible from aged and masculine vocal chords—and hung onto my arm screaming while I stared in helpless horror at his rotting yellow teeth and whitestubbled chin and mad, milky eyes, until two policemen pushed through the gathering crowd, detached him, and led him away.

It was a warm fall afternoon, with that rare, intense light you find only in cities where the sun (I may be imagining this) concentrates itself in the spaces between skyscrapers. Out of midtown, the light changes, becomes hazier and whiter and more expansive, and when the bus got to 60th Street, I got off, suddenly wanting to be out in it, and walked the rest of the way, up Fifth Avenue along the park. I met Pierce in New York for a weekend once, when he was in graduate school at Yale and I was living in southern Pennsylvania with my old roommate Bridget, working as a waitress, restless and unhappy, missing my uncomplicated college days. Pierce and I stayed in the Village, in a grungy little studio that belonged to a cousin of his who was out of town. We intended, finally, after all those years, to make love, but we got drunk and silly instead, and smoked too much pot, and ended up rummaging in the kitchen and eating cans of soup and sardines, then falling asleep on the floor, and the cousin and her boy-friend came back a day early, and we never did do what all our years of intimacy, Pierce said, had been leading up to. Instead we parted at the Port Authority, leaning against each other, unable to stop laughing at the weariness, the frustration, the comedy of it all.

And so New York, of course, always reminded me of Pierce, as so many things did, but, walking up Fifth Avenue in the sunshine, I made a big effort to forget about him and think about something else. By the time I got to the Frick I was doing quite well. I was thinking about Silvie, Emile's mother, whom I would see later. She had called me and invited me to lunch, as she did three or four times a year. She had said she wanted to talk about Denis. I always had trouble thinking coherently about my son, but I liked contemplating my ex–mother-in-law.

I had dressed the way I had for her sake. Sneakers and jeans were my usual costume, but Silvie liked women to wear skirts, and she didn't approve of sneakers except for running, and she didn't approve of running. I was wearing tights and Chinese slippers with a long, flounced, red-and-black plaid skirt and a black sweater, and I knew Silvie would like the way I looked. In spite of the divorce and what she (prompted by Emile) considered my ongoing instability, she continued in general to approve of me. She considered me, I think, quaint in a peculiarly American way. She liked it that I didn't wear fur or leather (though she wore plenty of both and was partial to blue fox, in which she looked fabulous) or make-up (in my forties I started wearing blusher and a little mascara, but she never noticed), and she liked my being a painter. She was especially happy that I didn't look "mainstream," the catch-all English word she had adopted to de-scribe, slightly inaccurately, what she considered dull or conservative. The first time she met James she told me afterward that he was "cer-tainly not a mainstream kind of fellow"—the word, with her accent, coming out something like "menstrim."

As I walked, I practiced my short collection of secure French phrases, recalled from one year of high school French and reinforced by six and a half years with Emile, so that I could use them on Silvie, who was charmed when anyone spoke French, however imperfectly, in her presence. *Bonjour, Silvie. Comment ça va? Il fait beau aujourd'hui, n'est-ce pas? Au revoir, Silvie. A la prochaine!* Emile had refused to speak French with me. He said my accent was terrible, but the real reason, I think, was that he wanted people to see me as hopelessly, provincially American so that by contrast he would appear even more cultured, more cosmopolitan, and (though he grew up in New York and, in those days, spoke English far better than he spoke French) more delightfully foreign than he really was. (He smoked Gauloises and even had a little goatee, and he occasionally tried on berets in stores, though he never went so far as to actually buy one.)

Silvie, however, told me my accent was quite good and I should cultivate it. I should travel to France. I should take a course. For all her chic, Silvie was very motherly, with a strong desire to improve people, to perfect them, and every time she saw me she made suggestions not only about my French but about my hair, my career, my relationship with James.

I was waiting to cross the street at the corner of 70th Street near the Frick, anticipating our conversation, figuring she wouldn't like my new haircut and trying to defend it in French (*"Mais bien sûr, Silvie, je doit porter mes cheveux comme je désire"*—no, that couldn't be right— *"Il faut que—"*), when from the knot of people at the curb a woman in a red coat broke loose and dashed diagonally across Fifth Avenue, waving something in the air and narrowly avoiding being hit by a car, crying, "Oh, Mr. Pierce—Mr. Pierce!"

A man on the other side of the street stopped, looked around as if bewildered (his back to me), and then the woman reached him, hung onto his arm for a second, and handed him a manila envelope. I could see her laughing face looking up at him—she seemed relieved, very glad to catch him—and then she turned away from him, hailed a taxi, which immediately pulled up to the curb, and got into it. He followed her, ducking fast into the taxi as if late for something, and they drove away. The light on my corner and, almost simultaneously, the next light down, at 69th, turned green, and the taxi drove on smoothly, unhampered, traffic lights obligingly greening before it as it proceeded down Fifth Avenue as far as I could see and disappeared behind a bus somewhere below 68th Street.

I stood stunned, unmoving, while the light turned green, then red again. My first thought was that I was hallucinating, and this idea in my mind crowded out what I really wanted to get hold of: could that have been Pierce? I didn't stop to ponder the irrationality of the question, I only tried to concentrate and bring back a picture of the man across the street. There was nothing to hang on to: he had been neither tall nor short, he wore some kind of trenchcoat, I couldn't even remember if it was the belted kind or not though I was sure it was tan, and he wore one of those shapeless, tweedy hats, the kind with a little curving brim all the way around, the kind designed to be folded up and shoved into a pocket. That was all I had seen. Not even his profile as he ducked into the cab, not even his hair color or the set of his shoulders. Neither tall nor short, neither fat nor thin, trenchcoat and hat: that was the best I could do. *I'm going crazy,* I thought.

Mechanically, I continued toward the museum when the light turned green again—moving with the crowd, entering between the tall doors, handing over my three dollars, and, somewhere in my consciousness, registering the particular atmosphere of the Frick—a museum that was like the splendid and imposing but oddly welcoming residence of one's filthy-rich great uncle. I headed, as I always did, past the marble pool with its twin spouting frogs and straight for the Bellini *St. Francis.* I wasn't thinking at all; my mind was blank. At most, I thought: *This is the Frick, walk this way to the Bellini.*

I stood in front of the painting, exhausted, as if I had come on a long journey. I would have liked to sit down, but I didn't want to leave the painting. I felt that if I looked at it long enough (something I loved, something outside myself) it would calm me down, bring me back to the real world: it would do for me what Charlie used to want music to do.

I looked at the painting: the mysteriously joyful saint in his rocky wilderness, the donkey, the sand-colored city in the distance, the shepherd, the lectern with its skull—and immediately Pierce entered my mind as if he had walked into the room, and I was filled with

Pierce-ness, pierced with the same sensation I had had twenty years ago in the grove of trees behind my parents' house.

It was the skull. On the extreme right of the Bellini painting, there is a roughly carpentered lectern; the saint's sandals rest beneath it, and on it are a red book and a skull—the skull, of course, a common motif in Christian paintings of the Renaissance (and after) for reminding us of our limitations, our certain progression toward the grave. I looked at it and immediately the blank screen of my mind filled with the picture of Pierce sitting on the floor of his tiny dorm room playing the guitar along with his favorite Big Bill Broonzy records. He was teaching himself to play, and he wasn't great, but he wasn't bad, either, and he was improving all the time. There were times, walking down the hall toward his room, when I'd hear Pierce playing and almost—almost—think it could be Big Bill, or Kokomo Arnold.

But he would get very depressed about his abilities, and I knew he was chagrined at not being able to excel at something he loved so much. Once when I walked in on him he was sitting there on the floor, the room full of clear yellow light the way the Bellini painting was full of light. He was working on some flashy runs (the kind of stuff Big Bill does in "Pig Meat Strut") and it was sounding pretty pathetic. When I walked in on him, he put down the guitar, leapt to his feet, and picked up the skull (stolen ages before from the biology lab) that he kept on his bookcase. He held it up and declaimed, "The last poor oryx. I knew him, Horatio"—one of his bad puns, the punchline to a long buildup about an African antelope called an oryx becoming extinct.

I'd heard the joke a dozen times (that and his *un, deux, trois, quatre, cinq* joke, about the three drowned French cats), and that particular occasion wouldn't, in fact, have stayed in my mind if it hadn't been for the way Pierce looked standing there in the light—like an earthier, more cynical St. Francis, the look on his face silly and rueful and intelligent and fond of me all at once.

I didn't mention the guitar-playing. I said, "I wish I had my sketch pad, you look great."

He said, "Damned right I do, and I should have had the fucking part, too." His rival in the Oberlin Dramatic Society, the devastating Jerry August, had played Hamlet the spring before; Pierce was Horatio, and it was one of those things he never got over. He hated Jerry, I have no doubt, until he died.

"Quit brooding over it."

"I'm the Hamlet type, brooding is my middle name. That's only one reason I should have had the part."

He replaced the skull on the bookcase, and then he put on a Roosevelt Sykes record, and we sat down to smoke a joint together. Gradually, the brilliant late afternoon light faded, and we went out somewhere or Charlie came in or someone else came in, I can't remember, it was just an ordinary day, but it came back to me (what he said, how he looked, the skull, the music) as I stood there at the Frick, so vividly that my knees felt weak and I had to leave the room and sit down out in the hall on a bench in front of the Ingres painting of the Comtesse D'Haussonville.

My mind cleared. I was vaguely aware of the gurgle of the fountain behind me, and of the maroon-suited guard, hands clasped behind his back, who was eyeing me in a concerned way—as if I looked not distracted but dangerous. I stared at the Comtesse, at her perfect, plump arm and her red hair-ribbon. She stared back at me with haughty interest. I thought of the woman on the train, Alison Kaye, and her appointment with Orin Pierce on Thursday. I saw the faceless, hatted man on the corner. Sentences fell into my consciousness like those brainteasers whose random pieces of information will, on examination, make up a perfectly logical statement:

Pierce never wore a hat in his life.

Pierce died in an accident in New Mexico twenty years ago.

For various reasons, including Silvie's desire to discuss Denis with me, I am in a mildly excitable condition today.

Twelve years ago, I had a vision of my brother Robbie.

Pierce loved me.

The conclusion, not logical, but necessary, that I drew from these facts was that Pierce was alive, he was in New York, and I had just glimpsed him wearing a hat and getting into a taxi on Fifth Avenue.

I took a deep breath and got up and made my way down the marble stairs to the women's room to bathe my face with cold water, and then I went back into the museum to look at Rembrandt's painting of the Polish rider.

Chapter Two

My *belle-mère* lived on Central Park West, in a building with a striped awning in front and a doorman dozing inside by the mailboxes. He ignored me. I took the elevator up to 8G and when Silvie opened the door, I said, "You know, Jack the Ripper could come up here with a knife dripping blood in each hand and your doorman wouldn't even notice."

She shrugged and said, not quite irrelevantly, "I've lived here twenty-four years." She gave me a hug and said, "Come in, darling."

"*Bon jour*, Silvie," I said. I pointed toward the window. "*Comment c'est beau au dehors! I mean, il fait beau, n'est-ce pas?*"

She stepped back to look at me. "I'm not sure about that haircut." She touched my hair, gingerly, and then my face, as if to be sure it was still me (round cheeks, brown eyes, freckles, Roman nose) under the crew cut. "I think you need more hair—for balance," she added—an enigmatic statement, but I knew what she meant (I am tall and big-boned), and imagined her thinking *pinhead* in French and trying to come up with the English equivalent.

"It was my hairdresser's idea," I said.

"I'm reserving judgment," said Silvie. "But I like your skirt very much. Mmm. . . . And that sweater is very good with the belt."

"*Comment ça va, Silvie?*" I asked her. "*Moi, je vais bien.*"

Lunch was ready, and we sat down to it: Silvie's usual canned soup and crackers, with celery sticks. Silvie couldn't be bothered with cooking. There were dozens of things she couldn't be bothered with: shopping, reading, going to movies, donating blood, giving dinner parties, having pets, taking photographs, sending Christmas cards, wearing a watch, finishing crossword puzzles. She was married to Fred Rafferty who, in spite of his name, was a professor of French literature at Columbia. Her first husband left her for a minor Swedish movie star, and his successor (Emile's papa) dropped dead of a heart attack, dramatically, on the Champs-Elysée when Emile was a toddler. She was fond of Fred, possibly because he worshipped her, and I believe she was very happy up there on the eighth floor in her luxury pad. But how she filled her time was a constant mystery to me.

"Put some crackers in that," she said to me, and I obediently crumbled a Ritz into my minestrone. We ate at a tiny table by the window in the cluttered, shabby living room (decorating and putting things away were two more things Silvie couldn't be bothered with) because the dining room table was covered with what Silvie called Fred's junk (his laptop, plus the books and papers and notecards he was using for his book on Stendhal) and the maid was out with the flu. Over the mantel through the French doors was one of my paintings, a large, semi-realistic watercolor of Central Park through Silvie's window that was very much like the view visible today: the trees in full, gaudy autumn bloom and beyond them a beautifully jagged grey-and-black skyline.

"The soup is good?" Silvie asked.

"It's very good."

"Maybe a bit on the salty side."

"No, it's fine."

"Well." She stopped to push her sleeves up her thin, bangled wrists, then said, "Denis is applying to Yale."

I was still thinking *soup*—used though I was to Silvie's hit-and-run method of conversation. "Yale?" I repeated, while I processed what she had said.

"Yes. He seems quite set on it."

Well, of course. It made perfectly good sense. In all his years living in New Haven teaching drawing and art history at a suburban art school, Emile's only contact with Yale had been his Sunday afternoons looking at paintings in the Yale Art Gallery, but, when people asked where he lived, he loved to say, "New Haven," and give his smug smile while the words "I'm at Yale, of course," hung silently in the air. He had revered the place, for no reason except that he was an outsider—a nobody—and also a snob. I was one of the few people on earth who knew that his degree was from a commercial art school in Albany.

"And what does Emile think of that?" I asked Silvie. I could see him passing his Yale hangup on to Denis, as he would pass on his taste in ties or his pronunciation of certain words, but I couldn't imagine him actually encouraging our son to return to the States, particularly to the city where I lived.

Silvie said, "Oh, he's all for it, believe it or not," and then she smiled. "Emile is in love. He's getting married again. A very nice young woman, twenty-nine, a dress designer."

I felt nothing—not jealousy, not chagrin, and not one *soupçon* of good will. There was no regret and no benevolence in my feeling for Emile. It had taken a while, but my only emotion toward my ex-*mari* was relief that he was gone. His French dress-designer chippie was welcome to him.

"And so he'd just as soon get rid of Denis?"

Silvie frowned. "I wouldn't put it quite that way."

"How would you put it?" I asked, and then I repented. "Oh, I know Emile is fond of Denis. And he spoils him rotten." Silvie smiled at this, approving. "I'm sure if Denis wants to go to Yale he's not going to forbid it. I'm just wondering what Emile thinks of Denis and me being in the same city. I mean, for twelve years he's done his best to keep us apart."

Silvie considered this. I could see her wondering if she should object to what I said, and deciding that it was fruitless. "I think he's reconciled to it," was what she finally said. "After all, Denis is nearly eighteen, and he's strong-minded."

"I can't believe he's old enough to go to college," I said—though it was one of those automatic, *tempus fugit* remarks, and not what I really felt at all. I had no trouble believing seventeen-and-a-half years had passed since the morning I gave birth to him, and nearly thirteen years had gone by since he had lived with me. Three years since I'd even set eyes on him. The time had passed swiftly, as time always does, but the years had been long nonetheless.

In those twelve years, I had seen my son three times: when he was eight, when he was ten, and when he was fourteen. I had talked to him on the phone only once—it hadn't worked out; we were both tongue-tied, and the connection was bad. But we had exchanged innumerable letters. *Dear Maman* and *Cher Denis,* over and over, at least one a week, since that first visit when he was eight. I still possessed every one of his letters, in his always improving but still eccentric and Frenchified English—from the laboriously printed early ones with their magic-marker pictures of dogs and spacemen, to the last several, typed on Emile's fancy new Macintosh. I kept them jumbled together in the capacious bottom drawer of my desk, and I got them out and reread them often: it was a constant source of refreshment to me, to open the drawer and choose a couple of letters at random and read them over before bed at night, or when I stopped painting to have a cup of tea, or when I was bored or unhappy or missing him, missing my baby, my beautiful young son.

I absorbed, very suddenly, the impact of what Silvie said. "And so he may go to Yale! My God, that's wonderful, Silvie, I can't believe it."

She smiled and patted her lips with her napkin. "If he gets in, of course."

"Do you think there's any doubt?"

"There's always doubt. Look at poor little Hilary." Hilary was Fred's granddaughter, who had her heart set on Harvard and ended up at SUNY Binghamton. "And Brian, out there in Minnesota breaking his heart." Brian, slightly less tragic, had gotten into Carleton but not Swarthmore. Fred had seventeen grandchildren, and Silvie had become an expert on the quirks of college admission requirements. "They say Yale is getting as choosy as Harvard. Fourteen per cent, that's all they take. And kids in America can take those SAT prep courses. There's nothing like that in Paris, darling."

"But Denis has done awfully well, Silvie. Plus he has his trumpet, the youth orchestra, all that. And I'm sure it's an advantage to be French. They like to have an interesting mix."

Silvie lowered her eyes and looked into her soup. I noticed, as I always did, how beautiful she was. Her eyelashes were impossibly long and curly, like insect legs; she had high cheekbones and a full, perfect mouth and a straight nose and coarse grayish-blonde hair done up in a messy bun. She was wrinkled, of course—she was sixty-something—but even her wrinkles were delicate and tasteful, as if someone who loved her had etched them, reluctantly, into the soft skin of her face. Emile looked nothing like her—his father must have been a dark, hairy, thin-faced, saturnine sort of fellow.

"What I wondered is if you know anybody," Silvie said, raising her blue eyes to my face.

"Know anybody where?"

"At Yale, Christine. In the admissions office."

"God, Silvie, I'm certainly not going to go down to Yale and try to convince them they should let my son in." But I would, I thought. I would if I could.

She sighed. "It's a dog-eat-dog world, Chris." An expression like dog-eat-dog sounded hilarious in Silvie's accent. "Without connections—" She gave her Gallic shrug. "*Rien.*"

"I have faith in Denis," I said, crumbling another cracker. "He'll get in. Where else is he applying?"

I thought, even if he ends up at Brown or Amherst or Columbia he'll be near me, and then while Silvie rattled on about the merits and demerits of various schools, I began to get cold feet. What if we didn't get along? What if he hated me when he got to know me? What if he came over here to school and refused to see me? Or saw me only out of a sense of duty? And why hadn't he written to me about his desire to go to Yale? Silvie had heard it from Emile: maybe he was spreading the rumor so that I would anticipate Yale and get slapped down with the Sorbonne or Grenoble.

"And I just don't think Oberlin would be right for him," Silvie said. "No offense, darling. But out in the middle of the midwest like that, after living in Paris. It would be worse for him even than for Brian, who after all is from Pittsburgh." She gave a little shudder. "I think Denis might find Ohio hard to survive."

We went on like that for a while, through the minestrone and the crumbled-up crackers, the celery sticks, the instant coffee and tangerines and Pepperidge Farm gingermen and—Silvie's little vice—the lunch-size snifter of Courvoisier.

"And now you're off to see this gallery man," she said to me at the door. "You're having a show in New York, that's so wonderful."

"I might be having a show. Someday. How did you know?"

She smiled archly. "I have my methods, don't I?"

"Really."

"Well—James told me."

"When were you talking to James?"

"Last night. I called him at the restaurant. I needed to know how you would take my news. I wasn't sure whether to tell you or not—about Denis. But James said you would take it very well, you would be thrilled. And so you are, I'm happy to see."

I said, "Silvie, I am not an invalid or a nut case. I have been a perfectly stable member of society for a long time. I'm in much better shape mentally than Emile ever was, believe me. I refuse to have you check up on me like that. What did you think I was going to do? Throw myself out the window? Go back to New Haven and plant bombs at Yale?"

Silvie smiled. "Christine, you are so extreme, *chérie*. Please. Don't blame me. I have only your welfare at heart. And don't blame James, certainly. He is so sweet. I made him swear not to tell you I called." It was true: James was the one I was angry at. He should have told me. Silvie laid a hand on my arm. "Don't be mad. It's just that everything is so difficult with you and Emile. Everything is so delicate."

"This has nothing to do with him," I said stiffly. "It's between me and Denis."

"Actually, as long as you're happy about it, it's between Denis and Yale, I'm afraid." She smiled dreamily. "Won't it be exciting? To have our boy right here with us?"

During the cab ride to the Aurora Gallery, I took out my wallet and looked at the latest photograph of Denis—a *lycée* picture. He wasn't smiling, he wore a white shirt and regulation tie, and his steady gaze was slightly mocking. I preferred candid shots of him, but I didn't get many of those: they would have involved Emile and his camera, and I could imagine him refusing to take photographs just so I couldn't have one. Denis had sent me one taken by a friend, of himself, in jeans and a t-shirt, straddling a bicycle. I had another, of Denis in a group of students in ski clothes, that Silvie had given me.

From what I could see, he had grown tall and broad-shouldered, and every time I looked at his photographs I was struck by his increasing resemblance to my brother Robbie.

~

George Drescher at the Aurora Gallery on Greene Street was a big fan of my work. A great watercolorist, he said, was rare—especially a painter like me, who had wonderful technique and didn't insist on applying it only to flowers and landscapes. George used to operate a gallery in New Haven—I was once in a group show there—and now he was trying to make a go of it in Manhattan.

He was succeeding, I thought when I walked in. The gallery was on the fourth floor of a landmark building, and it was pristine and bustling. George specialized in works on paper, and the show that was up was a series of startling woodcuts of ferocious, bejewelled animals—at least half of them bore tiny "sold" dots. I walked around and looked at them before I gave my name to the woman at the desk. George had asked me to come to New York so he could show me the actual physical space and we could discuss the possibility of my show-ing with him. He came to meet me with his arms outstretched as if a massive hug were coming up, but he only took my hand and shook it hard. "This is Christine Ward," he said to the woman at the desk (she was Japanese and anorexic, dressed in chic, shapeless black) as if I were a celebrity. The woman smiled at me blankly, and George hus-tled me into his office.

"So how are you, sweetie?" he asked. "What's new? What's going on in the provinces? What have you been up to?"

George's office was spare but expensive, with a table made of red marble, Italian-looking chairs, and what had to be a Picasso drawing on the wall. I felt slightly dazed from the events of the morning and the cognac at Silvie's and the luxury of George's gallery. His New Haven place had been located over a copy shop on Elm Street. "Oh, I don't know, George," I said. "I just found out my son is coming to Yale."

"Your son who lives in Paris?"

"That's the only one I've got."

"With the man who does those interesting illustrations—is that right? *Lucy's Dog.* Did I get it right?"

Lucy's Pup. Le Petit Chien de Lucie. Il Canino di Lucia. Das Hund von Lucy. The book that had transported Emile out of my life had been translated into thirteen languages and sold, in America, nearly 400,000 copies. It was incredible to me that a man as insensitive as I considered Emile to be could write such a wonderful book for children. Even I had to admit it was a wonderful book—a classic lost-and-found story of a little Parisian girl's search for her beloved doggie. Holding that book in my hands, I had wished desperately that I had a small child to read it to—tears came to my eyes with the desire to read that book to a child. Emile had been a moderately successful children's book illustrator for years; this was his first attempt at writing as well as illustrating, and it seemed to spark something in him: in the books he illustrated for others, the pictures were foggy and dreamy and formless—mysteriously unlike Emile's uptight personality, and unappealing, I always thought, to children, who tend to be literal-minded. But in his own book the drawings were crisp and charming and humorous, exactly right for the simple, timeless story. The book was an instant success. It came out just before Christmas the year that Denis was six, and it sold like crazy. Shortly after Emile left me, he was a rich man.

"That book had to make him a bundle," George said, and chuckled. "I just hope you got a piece of it."

"A bit," I said. Emile had gotten away with Denis, but until I began living with James he had paid me alimony—at Silvie's insistence, I always suspected. (I never did get a lawyer.) "Enough to allow me to paint on decent paper instead of on grocery bags."

"Well, thank heaven for that. I just wish you'd paint more. Here— I want you to see this." He put a slide in a machine at his elbow and projected it on the wall. It was one of the slides I had sent him—a self-portrait I had done a year ago: a shadow person, almost but not quite faceless, against a window. It was smaller than my usual paintings. George said, "This is the painting that epitomizes your work, Chris. I think it's a very strong, very dramatic piece, but it's also an accessible one, if you know what I mean." I did know what he meant: George was always telling me that my giant watercolors were too unusual for the marketplace. "It's also incredibly beautiful," he said.

"I mean, even aside from the subject."

He put his hand on my shoulder, caressing it lightly while we stood together and looked at the projection. I wondered fleetingly if George had designs on me. He was just my height, and probably my weight—a slight, blond, handsome man with a moustache. In New Haven, I had been friendly with his wife, Eva, a journalist who moved to Seattle after their divorce. "Watch out for George," she had said to me before she left. "He is never vanquished."

"This is such an intimate little thing," he said. "So warm. And it's reminiscent, somehow, of those early Georgia O'Keeffes, those little abstract watercolors. Before she got so full of herself. You know the ones I mean? This has the same reckless spirit. God, Christine, I wish you'd do more of this kind of thing."

Actually, the portrait made me uncomfortable—all my self-portraits did. Intimate seemed the wrong word: the paintings seemed phony to me, and confused; they revealed a self I didn't particularly like, one I had been trying for years to put behind me. They also seemed to me inexpressibly bad, and yet I couldn't stop painting them. The attempt was the important thing.

George kept right on rhapsodizing. "The delicacy that's so characteristic of your work is there, along with the incredible strength and vitality. And of course the size is perfect." He took his hand from my shoulder and pulled out a chair for me. We both sat down at the marble-topped table. "Really, I love it," he said. "I think it's this painting, of all of them, that says Christine Ward. That really shows us what you can do with your technique. What do you think?"

I shrugged. "It's fine. Sure." I didn't have the strength to argue with him, I would argue another time. "Are we really going to do this, then, George?" I asked him—out of a sense that he expected me to ask a practical question.

"We are most definitely going to do this, Christine," he said, and then sighed heavily. "But I need to see some more things from you, I don't want to stick you in a group. You know, when we do this, it's going to be a very big deal. We just might make you famous. Are you aware of that?"

"The idea seems pretty unreal to me," I said. This was true. I had had some success, mostly in various Connecticut galleries and with a rep I had had for years who managed to sell my larger pieces to corporations: bank lobbies, particularly, had a weakness for the large watercolors George said the gallery-going public wasn't ready for. I didn't really care what George thought. I wasn't ambitious. I painted because I liked to paint, and I couldn't imagine what else to do with my life. If I hadn't been able to pick up my brush and paint every day, I would have had nothing to live for.

"Are you okay, Christine?" George asked me. I could see why Eva had warned me, and why George was such a success with women. He was as attentive as a father. I could imagine that he was a skillful lover.

"I'm fine," I said.

George reached out and covered one of my hands with his. "You seem a little—" He shrugged. "Something." He turned my hand over and held it, smiling. "I worry about people who keep saying things are fine."

I let him hold my hand. I said, "I had an odd experience today. Two, actually. Twice I thought I had come into contact with someone I used to know. Someone dead."

"Someone you once loved?"

I nodded.

"That must mean you're unhappy in your personal life—now, today."

"I don't think I am, not really."

"But if your unconscious is so anxious to bring back the past—"

"It could just mean he's not really dead."

George frowned, squeezing my hand. "Be careful now, Christine. Don't get carried away. You hear what I'm seeing, sweetie? Let the dead rest in peace, don't dig them up."

His gruesome image recalled the movie *The Night of the Living Dead,* in which people who had recently died rose from their embalming tables to menace the living—eat their flesh, I seemed to remember. The movie was remarkable for the fact that there were no survivors, all the good guys were killed in the end.

"You think I'm imagining things," I said.

"Christine, if this person died, he died. There's no room for opinion here."

I wondered if he knew about my breakdown. No, that wasn't possible. I said, "He died out in New Mexico. It was so far away. I had a lot of trouble believing it."

"You didn't go to the funeral?"

"No—I never heard anything about it. I just buried myself at my parents' house and went around like a zombie for a whole summer."

He made a sympathetic noise. "It's like children, when their parents die," he said. "They say it's important that they go to the wake or whatever and actually see their parent dead, so that they can accept the reality of it."

"Yes," I said. I thought of Robbie in his closed coffin. "I suppose that would have helped."

We sat there in silence for a few moments, and somehow (I don't know how it happened, it was George's particular genius) the feeling between us changed from morbidity to lust. He rubbed my palm thoughtfully, absently, with his thumb. "You poor thing," he murmured. "You've had a rough day, haven't you?"

It was tempting to throw myself into his arms and say yes, yes, George, I've had a very rough day, and to let him take me out for a drink, dinner, and then to his apartment. I imagined the taxi ride there, frantic kissing, his hand between my legs, and then stumbling, pressed together, to the elevator, and attacking each other the minute we were inside his door. It would be different from what I had with James.

He rubbed my palm. I took a shaky breath and pulled my hand away. "It wasn't that bad," I said, standing up. "Actually, it's been a lovely day. The weather is incredible, and I had a very pleasant lunch with my ex–mother-in-law, and I got to see your gorgeous gallery." I gathered up my things—purse, *Swann's Way*, the bag of tangerines Silvie's friend had brought her from Florida and she had insisted on giving me half of. "And now I'll go home and eat one of James's fabulous pizzas for dinner."

George gave me a kind, knowing smile. Implied in it was: *you don't know what you're missing,* but also: *I respect your wishes, and your flawed personal life that is making you unhappy, epitomized by your insane commitment to a weird pizza-maker.*

"There are only two things I miss about New Haven," George

said. "The pizzas at Jimmy Luigi's and you." He took my hand again and gazed into my eyes. "Go home and paint, Christine. Send me more slides. I want you in my gallery."

And then there was the train ride home, and one of Silvie's tangerines, and *Swann's Way*—just a few more pages, into the Combray section that sprang from Marcel's fateful cup of tea. I read a bit, looked out the window at the nothingness along the tracks in the dark, read a bit more. I took out Denis's photo and looked at it again, and I brought into my mind the self-portrait George had projected on the wall, and I compared our two round, high-nosed, freckled faces. I thought of the Bellini *St. Francis* at the Frick, and the skull, and the odd and unpleasant sensation of actually feeling faint, of feeling your knees buckle and having to sit down quickly before you sink to the floor in a heap. I thought about Denis's chances of getting into Yale, and about *Lucy's Pup,* and about having a show at the Aurora. At Stamford, I thought about the yuppie, Alison Kaye of Haver & Schmidt, and her appointment with Olive Pounce, and I thought about the man in the trenchcoat and his squashed hat that was unlike anything Pierce would ever wear. I read some more *Swann's Way,* about Françoise gossiping with Marcel's aunt, and about the old church where Marcel went to Mass with his parents.

Then I was in New Haven, and James was there to meet me. I was so glad to see him, I couldn't be angry about his talk with Silvie, and at Jimmy Luigi's I swore to myself, I swore that I would keep myself from going crazy if it was the last and hardest thing I did.

Chapter Three

I'd been living with James for almost three years, and during that time Jimmy Luigi's had prospered. James had taken a chance, just before he moved in with me, and relocated his place from out in Westville to downtown New Haven. New Haven was dying, everyone knew that; the politicians said it could be saved if people would just do their civic duty and go downtown and shop until they drop; the editorial writers said it could be saved if the politicians were more responsible; some said it could be saved if the media didn't give it such a bad rep. Everybody thought Yale should pitch in. James thought all it needed was a really good downtown pizza parlor.

James Lewis, a WASP accountant from Baltimore, was reborn into Jimmy Luigi, a New Haven pizzateur (his word). I wasn't even clear about how the transition came about. It had something to do with a woman he followed to New Haven (she taught at Yale Law School) and her eventual spurning of him, but there was much more to it than that—James was too unusual to change his life for anything so straightforward as unrequited love. He became disillusioned with what he called the raving idiocy of his work (he claimed he turned against accountants from watching Monty Python) and ran a soup kitchen for a while, and then he tutored inner-city kids in math, and then he worked in a pizza place that was cooperatively run as a socialist experiment, and then he worked in a regular pizza place, and then he decided to open his own out in Westville, and then he relocated to downtown New Haven and the rest is history.

I met him because I got addicted to white clam pizzas during the winter after Denis's last visit to me. Denis spent Christmas with me in New Haven, and I was so depressed when he went back to France that all I could do was eat: nothing but food gave me any comfort. But I couldn't cook for myself. It wasn't that I couldn't be bothered, like Silvie. I love to cook, even when I'm depressed—in fact, nothing cheers me up like getting into the kitchen with my sleeves rolled up—but I kept burning everything. I couldn't keep my mind on what I was doing. I couldn't stop thinking about Denis's cheerful leave-taking, about how clear it was that he might be fond of me but he was crazy about Emile and his life with him in Paris. About how French he was, how so many things in America had aroused his scorn or amusement. (He was fourteen, a scornful, amused age.) I burned rice, I burned eggs, I burned oatmeal and broccoli and frozen Italian dinners. My smoke detector kept going off. My neighbors kept either complaining about me or worrying about me, until finally I stripped my kitchen down to apples and milk and cold cereal, and went out every night for dinner.

I was living in Westville then, in an apartment house on Alden Avenue—three gloomy rooms and a very sad bathroom. I was working as a receptionist in a dentist's office, where I had to wear a white uniform and white stockings like the ones the perky half-my-age hygienists wore. Dr. Mankoff liked us to keep our skirts at knee-length. (I once heard him say to someone on the phone, "I pick my girls for brains first, legs a close second.")

My cat, Mabel, had died of kidney failure just before Denis came for Christmas. She had been our cat when Denis was little. He didn't remember her very well, but I always associated Mabel with Denis's childhood. He had learned to crawl by lunging across the rug after her, and one of his first words was "teetat." When he left, and Mabel wasn't there either, I was hit hard by the loss.

After work, when the bus let me off on Whalley Avenue, I almost always ate dinner at one of the restaurants there, and my favorite place was Jimmy Luigi's. I would go there three or four times a week, order a small white clam special, and have a beer while I waited and another beer while I ate. The pizza made a good cheap dinner, with a couple of extra pieces to take home for the next day's cold lunch, and the two beers were just the right amount to dull my various griefs and put me to sleep at night.

James was usually behind the counter making the pizzas. I was vaguely aware that he was Jimmy Luigi himself, though I never heard anyone call him anything but James, and I liked him a lot, instinctively, before I fell in love with him or really knew him. Even then, before he made a lot of money, he was overweight—not grossly, not unattractively (he's big and heavy-boned, like me, and he can stand a few extra pounds), but definitely overweight. I assumed he was Italian: the pizzas, the name, the big black moustache. I could see him growing up in East Haven. I could see his wife, probably a petite dark-eyed schoolteacher named Joanne, and his two clean-cut kids (Jimmy Jr. and Jennifer), a nice old matriarchal mother, half a dozen brothers and sisters all living in the same neighborhood, and a pool table and built-in bar in the basement of his split level.

I'm not totally unperceptive: that's the guy James would have been in an ideal world. Instead, he was an only child and an orphan and a burned-out C.P.A. His ex-wife Nona was a pediatrician in Baltimore. They had no children, which was one reason they split up. He lived on Avon Street in a third-floor apartment huddled so closely under the eaves that all the rooms were triangular. He was almost as lonely as I was.

I didn't actually meet him until I showed up one night for dinner and saw a big sign in the window that said Jimmy Luigi's was closed for a month and would reopen downtown on Chapel Street. I couldn't believe it: not only was my neighborhood pizza parlor deserting me for good, but I had been looking forward all day to my white clam special and two beers. Rituals were important to me. I didn't have a lot of friends, I had almost no time to paint, my feelings about my job ranged from boredom to loathing, my only child lived three thousand miles away and spoke a foreign language, my cat was dead. Jimmy Luigi's was one of the few stable, positive elements in my life. I went up the street to the Chinese place and had a greasy egg roll, vegetable fried rice that tasted canned, and so much tea that I couldn't sleep at all that night.

In those days, I was just getting into the oversized watercolors that would eventually become my trademark, if I had a trademark, and painting was more real to me than anything. The weekends would fly by while I worked. I had my rituals. Friday night, no matter how tired I was, I prepared the large surfaces on which I would work: I cut the paper from the huge roll I had bought instead of winter boots, soaked it in the tub, made stretchers and stapled the paper tight, like a white rectangular drum. By Saturday morning, when it was dry, I could start. Often, I hadn't had enough sleep—the excitement and anticipation would keep me awake—and I would enter the sparse morning light of the room where I worked, impatient to get going, and be paralyzed by the perfection of that expanse of white. How could I possibly improve it? What could I bring to this rare purity? And then the reluctance would pass and I would feel the adrenalin course through me, and I would squeeze out my colors, fill the two Mason jars with water, sketch in the outlines, and begin the initial wash. Time would pass, and the next thing I knew it was dark out, I was faint with hunger, and before me there was the rough beginning of a painting that filled me with a combination of rapture and dread. Sunday would be the same. I discovered that it was possible to finish a 40 x 60 inch painting in a weekend if I worked fourteen hours at a stretch.

Getting into my white uniform and stockings every Monday morning was like putting on prison garb, but all day Monday I would remain in a state of exhilaration. This wore off by the evening, and for the rest of the week things were at the point where my nightly beer and pizza were the high point of my life. I began to anticipate them around 2:00 every day.

The day after I saw the sign in the window of Jimmy Luigi's, I went down to the new place on Chapel Street and looked in the window. It was an unpromising little ex–shoe store a couple of blocks up from the Green. The windows were still filthy, but inside I could see men working. I thought I caught a glimpse of James, so I banged on the window. One man looked up from what he was doing and motioned me irritably away, but I banged again, and James finally came over, peered through the window, and came outside to see what I wanted.

It was freezing out, with a brutal wind whistling up Chapel Street, between the buildings, from the Sound. I felt bad dragging him out in the cold, and once I had him there I wasn't sure what to say. All the way down, I had been thinking of the Hemingway story, "A Clean, Well-Lighted Place," and how much like that old man I felt. I suppose I had intended to reproach James for leaving the neighborhood, to tell him how I had depended on him and what a hole his leaving would put in my lousy little life.

"May I help you?" he said. His voice was kind. He wore earmuffs and a ski jacket. He looked like a bear. I just stared at him. "Can I do something for you?"

I pulled myself together and said, "I used to eat out at your place in Westville."

"Yeah, I thought you looked familiar." He stuck his hands in his pockets and puffed out his cheeks and rocked back and forth on his heels, the way people do when they're cold.

"It was really great pizza," I said.

"It's going to be even better down here," he said. "You wait and see."

"I don't get downtown that much, really."

"You will." He smiled at me. "You'll come down for Jimmy Luigi's." He looked like he wanted to leave, but he added, with dogged politeness, "Was there something I could do for you?"

I felt I owed it to him to say something else, he'd been so nice about coming outside to talk. "Well, my cat died," I said. I meant that to be the beginning of a concise litany of my woes, culminating in my personal reaction to the loss of Jimmy Luigi's, but after I said it I couldn't go on, I couldn't lay my troubles on such a nice man, and so I said, "But it doesn't matter, I don't want to bother you, I just wanted to say I'll miss having your place right down the street from me. I really like your white clam pizza. I like the oregano especially."

But he wasn't listening. He was frowning off into space, grimacing slightly, running his hand over his jaw and around to the back of his neck—portrait of a person thinking. He said, "Let me think, let me just think."

"Really," I said. "I don't mean to keep you out here." I gestured vaguely up Chapel Street. It was winter-bleak, the whole city was, all of southern New England was grey and ugly, most of the snow melting as soon as it fell, the endless traffic churning up what was left, the air smelling of chemicals and exhaust and damp, and people on the street, chased by the wind, looking red-nosed and desperate and drugged-out on cold medications. I said, "I was just on my way up to—"

"Wait," he said. "I'm thinking. How would you like a pair of them?" I looked at him. He had greenish-brown eyes that were very, very slightly crossed, and his front teeth were very, very slightly crooked. I didn't know what he meant. Pizzas? He said, "How about a couple of nice red tabbies?"

It turned out he ran a cat-placement service on the side. He didn't keep the cats himself; his friend Hugh had a barnful out in Southbury, and James was always on the lookout for potential adoptions. He placed an average of ten cats a month, he said, but the cats kept multiplying, he couldn't keep up. The two tabbies, though, had belonged to James and his ex-wife, Nona. She had remarried and had a baby and the baby was allergic to the cats, and so the cats had come to James and were now with Hugh. James couldn't keep cats in his tiny, triangular place, and besides he was never home, which wasn't fair to a pet. Their names were Rosie and Ruby, short for Roseola and Rubella. "We thought that was clever because my wife is a pediatrician," James said. "Now I just think it's stupid. She still thinks it's clever. She and her new hubby got a gerbil for the baby and named it Dr. Spock, ha ha. But Rosie and Ruby are great cats—identical twins, six years old, neutered, affectionate, gorgeous, clean, fluffy, outgoing, intelligent, temperate in their habits . . ."

I agreed to take the cats. James smiled and shook my hand, and we went up to Claire's for herb tea and huge slabs of Hungarian coffee cake. We talked about our awful exes. James ordered a second piece of cake. I loved watching him eat, he ate with such unself-conscious enjoyment. I thought I had never seen such a contented man, and without his down jacket he wasn't really all that huge.

Rosie and Ruby moved in with me the next day, and James two weeks later, and the new Jimmy Luigi's opened on Valentine's Day and was a smash hit from the beginning. I quit my job with Dr. Mankoff. James showed me how to keep the books for Jimmy Luigi's and then dumped everything in my lap. He hated that part of it—his old profession. He wanted only to make pizza. Sometimes I helped out on Friday and Saturday nights, working alongside Jimmy and his chief assistant Raymond in the hot kitchen. I grew to love the heat, and the good-natured insults, and the clean, redstained aprons we all wore, and the overpowering smells of tomato and oregano and yeast. I learned how to flatten a ball of dough and twirl it into a circle, but I could never make mine as thin as James's. What I liked best was removing the finished pizza from the oven with a long-handled wooden paddle, flipping it onto a metal tray, and slicing it—zip zip zip—into perfect eighths.

And that's all there is to say about my life with James. We were a phenomenon: two people who managed to be happy together. It was that simple, and after the complexities of life with Emile, simplicity was what I was looking for.

～

I did my best to put Alison Kaye and her Filo-Fax out of my mind, but I didn't succeed. All day Wednesday, I was conscious that the next day was Thursday, and that her lunch date at Chez D. was for 1:30, but I didn't let myself do any of the things I wanted to do, which ranged from getting out all my old pictures of Pierce and studying them with a magnifying glass to making frantic phone calls to try to locate Haver & Schmidt or Chez D. or Alison Kaye herself. Consequently, I did nothing. James was working, and I was supposed to be painting and doing laundry. I sat around all day staring out the window at the wind ripping the leaves off the trees in our back yard.

On Thursday morning, I woke with a sense of urgency, still gripped by the violent and bloody atmosphere of a dream I could mercifully remember nothing about. As soon as James left for work at eleven, I gathered together all my photographs of Pierce. There weren't many. His official college photo in the Oberlin yearbook, a candid shot (taken at a picnic) also in the yearbook, the photo of the two of us (in color, with red eyes) in front of his apartment building, and another photo (black and white, and rather murky) of Pierce and two guys he knew in drama school wearing huge straw hats and serapes and holding guitars and grinning insanely.

I got the rectangular magnifying glass out of the little drawer at the top of the compact edition of the Oxford English Dictionary (the boxed set, which Emile had purchased in 1976 when the Book of the Month Club had a good deal on it—when I was in the Yale–New Haven psychiatric ward learning to make baskets). I couldn't look at the OED without resentment—that my husband had been so undisturbed by my troubles that he could perform the prosaic act of ordering from the Book of the Month Club a two-volume, 4000-page dictionary in a language he was making secret plans to repudiate along with his wife. In fact, he left the dictionary behind when he took off with Denis for France, and I would have given it to the book sale along with Proust except that it was too heavy to carry.

I looked at the graduate school photograph first, because Pierce was wearing a hat—I thought I might catch a hint of the Mr. Pierce in the hat by the Frick. But all I could see was my Pierce: close up, how white his teeth were (I remembered them as yellowish), what a smile he had, how his hair hung in his face. And, from a detective's point of view, how nondescript he was—an ordinary guy, neither handsome nor ugly, not big, not little, no distinguishing features, no visible quirks. Anyone asked to describe him would think only: average, Everyman, John Q. Public.

I looked at the other photographs. The college portrait didn't resemble him much (jacket, tie, set jaw, steely eyes), though it could have been his duller, straighter, handsomer older brother if he had had one. The candid picnic shot showed him bent over a cooler of what was probably illegal beer, glancing over his shoulder with an enigmatic look that, on examination, could have been either quizzical or irritable. He was overshadowed by a blonde girl in shorts who stood posing with her hand on her hip—Judy somebody, I vaguely recalled. Judy somebody's legs were undoubtedly the reason the photograph was included—Pierce was incidental.

The photo of Pierce and me was the best. We were about the same height, and we were dressed similarly in jeans and jackets. He was hatless, looking straight into the camera with his characteristic expression—a crooked, dubious smile—but he was also squinting into the sun, and so his face, less clear than it could have been, was distorted into a mild grimace. (Beside him, I'm looking down at my shoes, and as I stared at Pierce's sunstruck face and the meek-looking top of my head, I vaguely recalled being furious with both him and Charlie—who took the picture with his Instamatic—though the reason why eluded me. The best I could dredge up was that Pierce had said something that angered me, and Charlie had laughed at my anger, and that the whole silly dispute hadn't lasted very long.)

I looked at the photograph, into Pierce's red, squinty eyes, remembering him and knowing at the same time that my memory was unreliable. I knew he had had thick brown hair, amused eyes whose real color I couldn't recall, an ironic smile, thin hands with wide nails, a touch of post-adolescent acne on his neck. I had tried many times to draw him when I was taking Emile's watercolor course (that was how we met—Emile was my painting teacher), and had realized then that I would never get him right. I was appalled at how little I had observed in all those years when I saw him constantly: I couldn't recall the shape of his face, or his ears, or even what his nose was like or the exact configuration of his mouth beyond the characteristic smile. I tried again, sitting at the kitchen table with the photographs. Even with their help, the drawings I attempted of Pierce were like those composite sketches of crime suspects you see in the newspaper: improbable-looking, somehow—the face not of a real person but of some alien being who resembles a real person.

I thought: what if I did show up at 1:30 at Chez D. to confront Orin Pierce as he lunched with Alison Kaye? Would I even recognize him? Twenty years had gone by; he could be anything: obese, crippled, scarred, bald, an uptight businessman in a pin-striped suit, a Republican politician, a slick-haired super-salesman, a flashy big shot with a gold chain around his neck and his hairy chest exposed. He could have had a sex-change operation, could be wearing a dress and pearls: Olive, Orina, Odessa. He could have had plastic surgery (big nose, buck teeth, hollow cheeks) and gone into the CIA as a spy. I couldn't even guess what he'd be eating for lunch. Pierce used to like chili, I remembered, and Twinkies. He liked apples: he and I once ate apples sitting on a wall somewhere talking about some movie. He drank his coffee black. He liked cherry pie and Ma's Old Fashioned Root Beer. And the question was, even if he looked exactly the same and sat there in Chez D. in his old brown corduroys and filthy Oberlin sweatshirt eating chili and Twinkies, would I recognize him?

I crumpled up the sketches I had made. I had lost him, it was like having him plunge off that cliff all over again. Who didn't like cherry pie? Who didn't eat apples? There were a million people who wanted to be great blues guitarists, a zillion with crooked smiles, a million zillion who could harmonize with the Everly Brothers. And that was all I had—a few hoarded moments, a few facts, a smile. It was nothing—nothing. Somehow, over the years, Pierce had disappeared. What I remembered was no more than what I remembered from my dream the night before: an atmosphere, a feeling, a foggy unreliable aura that meant *Pierce* to me.

It was nothing. He was dead.

Chapter Four

I knew that I needed to free myself. I knew that what I saw on the train and outside the Frick were like specks of dust that, however tiny, could stick my life in a groove when what it needed was to keep moving forward. I had to eliminate the schemes going through my head: get in touch with Alison Kaye, start calling old friends, look up the newspaper stories of Pierce's death and get the details—all of which, I was aware, presupposed that Pierce wasn't dead at all but that he had staged his own death like Huckleberry Finn, or contracted amnesia, or assumed another persona for purposes of his own, or lost his reason. If I didn't stop myself I would imagine him living in New York, lunching at Chez D., doing business with people like Alison Kaye, walking the streets in his trench coat and tweedy hat. Passing me, perhaps, and recognizing me, but choosing not to speak. Recalling me only vaguely, and not with affection but with revulsion, with hostility. Glad to be dead to his old life. Glad to be this new improved Pierce, unencumbered by memory.

I gathered up my Pierce artifacts, dumped my needlepoint yarn out of the picnic basket, and packed them into it. I put the basket on the shelf—high and hard to get at, with shoeboxes stacked on top of it, the way James on a diet would stash the taco chips in the highest reaches of the pantry.

All that fall, I concentrated on forgetting.

I had been working on the series of self-portraits, even though I didn't think they were going well. Now and then I had achieved a glimmer of what I wanted to do: a window into some future state where everything I painted would express what I wanted it to express and no more—a state that is probably not achievable for an artist but for which I felt I had to strive.

But I had to give up on these portraits. They were getting away from me. They began to resemble Denis strongly, and Robbie, and the more I worked on them, the more I kept trying to see Pierce's face and finding it impossible to see my own. The end result was that I saw nothing clearly, and the images I produced were vague, formless, flat, and cold, with a disturbed edge to them that recalled Emile's abuse of me when I split up, the things he said while I was in the hospital learning to make baskets and crying all the time. At the end of every day, I would look at the dismal load of work I had produced and feel desperate: the day was gone, unrecoverable, and all it had brought me were these sad, inept paintings of no one and nothing.

I began painting still lifes of pottery and fruit and books and teacups. I did fussy, detailed views of the trees and rooftops out my studio window. These were subjects that I had learned to turn to as a refuge when I needed one, all of them the conventional things that George would hate but that I hoped I could justify with my famous technique. And at least they achieved their purpose, which was quite simply to distract me from that day in New York.

Denis finally wrote me a letter about his application to Yale. Denis always wrote in English (though Emile discouraged it), and his English, which deteriorated as soon as Emile got him to France, was charmingly odd. He wrote: "The only thing that hesitates me about making this application is that you might wish not to have me in town so closely. Maybe a nearly grown son so near to your premises would not be what would be best for you. I count on you to tell me this honestly." Behind these worries I detected the hairy hand of Emile and I wrote immediately to Denis assuring him that I wanted nothing more than to have him near to my premises. Emile as a father, it often seemed to me, had a great deal in common with the Secret Service, which guards the president so closely that he can't lead anything resembling a normal life.

At Christmas, James and I packed up the cats in their carriers and went to visit my parents. We'd been doing that every year, spending two full weeks, during which Jimmy Luigi's was run by James's apprentice, Raymond Dudley, one of the ghetto kids James had once tutored and continued to take a personal interest in. Raymond sometimes got creative with the pizza (he was a great believer in hot sauce, and he thought the white clam special was improved by a touch of rosemary), but he was reliable, and his annual two-week stints as manager and "primo pizzateur" were, James said, like his final exams. He'd been doing it for three years; one more year, and he'd have what James called his Bachelor of Pizza degree.

My father was eighty-four, and his health was beginning to fail. He slept most of the time. He hardly ever talked, but that was nothing new. James called him Pop, even when he didn't get a response. He called my mother Ma Ward, which for some reason charmed her. She was seventy-seven, and livelier than I remembered her in her younger days. She looked forward to my visits with James so much that I don't think it ever occurred to her to disapprove of our living together.

James loved it that my parents lived in a town called Jamesville: he mailed all his Christmas cards from the post office there. My mother and father had operated a prosperous motel on Route 92. I lived all the years of my youth in a big old house behind the row of cottages. The motel had been closed for fifteen years, and the cottages where I spent my summers changing the sheets and scrubbing out the sinks with Bon Ami were picturesque, termite-ridden shacks my mother talked about tearing down. Every year I did bright, abstracted paintings of them—little ones, George would have loved them: the cottages fenced around with snow, their old bare boards turned into gold by the sun. Behind our house was the grove of trees—my comfort the summer Pierce died— and beyond that was a small, shallow pond where Robbie and I had ice-skated as children.

Now James and I skated there. He was a terrific skater, graceful on his feet and inventive, full of tricky moves. On the ice, he could jump over a log, twirl in midair and land facing it, then skate rapidly backwards. If he had enough space, he could skate his initials—a florid, loopy J.L. He taught me to waltz on skates and to play a modified form of ice-hockey designed for two players. My mother, one of the

cats draped over her shoulder, would watch us from the big picture
window in the back parlor, and when she considered that we had
been out there long enough or it began to get dark, she would appear
on the back steps, waving, and calling, "Cocoa's ready!" Like a
mother in a book, she would have cocoa waiting for us, and cookies
right out of the oven, just as she did when Robbie and I were little. She
never mentioned Plover Island, or Robbie's name, but I always considered ancient rituals like the cocoa, and her face at the window watching James and me on the ice, to be silent tributes to my brother's
memory.

I got a Christmas card from Charlie. He always sent me cards at
my parents' place, when he sent them at all, because he could never
be sure of my address. James and I, in fact, had bought a jaunty little
Victorian house on Bishop Street in New Haven—narrow and heavily gingerbreaded—that we'd painted in the kind of San Francisco
colors that were all the rage in our neighborhood: three shades of
high-gloss blue with touches of dark green, magenta, and brilliant
yellow—possibly too whimsical, too cute, but we loved it. I hadn't
yet sent Charlie the address. According to the note on the back of his
card (a roguish Santa unloading his pack), he was still in L.A., still
working for the agency, and he was involved with a woman who, he
said, just might work out. At the end of his note, he wrote: "It was
twenty years last summer that Pierce died. Isn't that incredible? I still
can't accept it that he's dead. I wish I could see you. Maybe next time
I'm in N.Y."

The last part I didn't pay much attention to: he said pretty much
the same thing every time he wrote, and yet we never got around to
meeting. But I read over and over the sentence, "I still can't accept it
that he's dead." Accept it. What did he mean by that? Did it mean he
literally didn't believe it? That he suspected Pierce of being alive?
That he had some evidence? Had he—my heart caught when I
thought of this—had he, perhaps, caught a glimpse of Pierce somewhere? Had he had a vision similar to mine?

I had decided to tell James nothing of my New York experience.
What was there to tell? And even if there were more substance, James
was so—I have trouble coming up with the proper adjective—he
was so normal (but that sounds dull), he was so cheerful (but that

makes him seem mindless), he was so perfect the way he was that I hesitated to introduce trouble into his life. Not that he hadn't had plenty of troubles. He'd had a more than usually difficult childhood (orphaned young, no siblings, raised by unsympathetic aunts), his marriage had been turbulent, the discovery that he couldn't father children had devastated him, and after his divorce he'd had some rough relationships before he met me. But he was like someone out of Dickens—Oliver Twist, perhaps, who maintained his sweet nature and optimistic spirit no matter what horrors he endured—or like Proust himself, in his cork-lined room, working furiously against the deadline of death but never losing his serenity of soul. I thought of James as a saint, a St. Francis, a savior not only of cats and of kids like Raymond but of myself. He was a being of contagious contentment, and I needed that quality in him more than I needed to confide what happened in New York.

Charlie had enclosed one of his business cards. He was with the Harlan Vickery Agency, and their card—much less elegant and classy than Alison Kaye's—was dominated by a big red-and-blue HV monogram/logo that looked like it had been designed in 1953. I wondered if it was consciously kitschy or if it simply hadn't been changed in all those years. Down in the left corner was *Charles Molloy* in blue and in the right corner a Los Angeles phone number in red.

I studied the card, and the Christmas card with the smirking Santa, and I pondered Charlie's choice of words (*I still can't accept it that he's dead*), and I couldn't keep from wanting to phone him. I needed to talk about it with someone—not James, not anyone who hadn't known Pierce, there was no one but Charlie I could tell it to. It wouldn't let me go. *I tried,* I justified myself to an imaginary accuser—a Satanic presence (not unlike Emile) who said I was pandering to my own mental instability, encouraging it. But it was true that I had tried. I had been stern with myself, had banished it all from my mind and hidden it away in a closet, only to find it emerging in my painting, in visions of the Satanic accuser, and in my violent, unremembered dreams. Being at my parents' house didn't help, of course—the grove of trees, the reminders of Robbie and of the time that Pierce and I spent there before we all drove up to Plover Island that summer.

I wasn't sleeping well. The elusive, nightmarish dreams I was having made me wake up before dawn. But one night I slept straight through and had a very clear and insistent dream in which I was talking to a psychiatrist—not Dr. Dalziel, the one I saw after my breakdown, but someone else, someone I didn't know, who said: "Call Charlie, you need to face this."

I called the next afternoon—morning, California time—a few days after Christmas, when James and my mother were out at the supermarket and my father was upstairs napping. I didn't have any other phone number, so I called him at the agency—half wishing he'd be out of town or hadn't come in yet. But he was there, and I gave my name, and he answered instantly.

"Chris! God, it's great to hear from you. What's up?"

We said the usual things: How nice to get his Christmas card, James and I were vegging out at my parents', he was taking a week off in January to go to Hawaii with his new girlfriend, blah blah. We compared L.A. weather with Jamesville weather, and then we ran out of topics, and I said, "Actually, Charlie, I wanted to tell you about something that happened to me, I wanted to get your opinion."

"Sure," he said. "Shoot."

I told him about the two incidents in New York. As I said them aloud, actually told them to a real person, they didn't sound crazy and improbable as I'd feared they would: they sounded amazing, convincing, a little scary. I could sense that Charlie, across three thousand miles, was impressed, was being persuaded against his will.

"Jesus, Chris," he said when I was done.

"Yes," I said.

"It's weird."

I said, "Charlie—what you said on your card, that you still can't accept his death. Did you really mean that? I mean—have you ever had any doubts about it? Have you ever thought he didn't really die?"

He took his time answering, and I imagined him (red hair thinning, sleeves rolled up) in his office (a window framing palm trees and unimaginable sunshine, a cluttered desk piled high with books and movie scripts), frowning into the phone, intent on this bizarre phone call that certainly wasn't what he'd expected on a Thursday morning. And in his mind would be his own memories of Pierce, and the evening when he climbed my stairs and wept and said, "Pierce is dead."

"Hell, Chris, I don't know," he said at last. "I don't think I ever thought that, not that concretely. I can't say I meant it literally—just that, I don't know—" He gave a little laugh. "You get to be middle-aged, and you get thinking, I think about that stuff a lot more now than I did when I was younger. I mean, I really miss Pierce. And you. I miss you both. I guess I'm missing myself, if you know what I mean. Being young. We were all such buddies. You know?"

His voice had thickened. I had tears in my eyes. Dear old Charlie. It often seemed to me that Pierce and I had underestimated him, that he was the best of the three of us. I remembered the time, when Charlie was being especially stubborn about something, that Pierce (who was rehearsing for *Becket*) had murmured, "Will no one rid me of this turbulent Charles?" A joke, but Charlie was horribly hurt, and it had bothered me for years that I did nothing to comfort him. Even now, I wanted to say, "He didn't mean anything by it, it was just something he tossed off to show how clever he was, it had nothing to do with you personally."

I waited a moment and said, "But don't you ever think he might not have been in that car?"

"Oh, Christ, it was his car, Chrissie," Charlie said, his voice under control. "They found his driver's license on him—on the body."

"But Charlie, you know how Pierce was—the kind of mood he was in that spring. He'd gotten so crazy, and he was always high on something, he'd been dropping a lot of acid. He could have done anything—lent someone his car and his license—hell, Charlie, he could have given them away if he was in the right mood."

"They did a positive identification, Chris. I'm not sure how, actually. The bodies were—well, you know what they said. And the car was down in that canyon or whatever for days. I mean, no one ever questioned it, not that I know of. But there were animals out there. I don't know how much was actually—" He paused. "Actually left."

"God."

"Yeah."

"Well—can't you see that there's a chance that Pierce wasn't there?"

"I suppose I'd have to grant you that—I mean, not knowing the details, I assume the police, the labs—I assume the positive identification had to have been based on something concrete, Chris."

"But suppose that it wasn't, that the identity was just taken for granted—"

"Well then, what bothers me is where is he?"

"He's in New York," I said. "He's become some kind of big executive." I tried to laugh. "He wears a hat, Charlie. He has lunch with people who carry briefcases."

"But why didn't he get in touch with us? Why is he in hiding? Why wouldn't he come forward, Chris?" He laughed too. "I mean, no one wants to be considered dead unless they've committed a crime or something."

My mind closed down over that. I said, "I admit this is strange, Charlie. I don't have any answers. So far I just have these questions."

"So far. That sounds like you're going to do something."

"I want to do something. I feel I have to. I just don't know what."

"Call his mother out in Michigan."

"Oh—right: Hi, Mrs. Pierce, remember me, did it ever occur to you that Orin is alive and living in Manhattan? Not dead, only resting."

"You wouldn't have to put it like that, you could be a little more roundabout."

"Actually, I thought I'd start a little closer in. I thought I'd get in touch with that woman."

"The woman on the train?"

"Sure. Why not? I know where to find her. And what have I got to lose?"

"Christine—" I heard Charlie strike a match and inhale. It surprised me that he still smoked, and I had the sense that he was trying to quit, had wanted a cigarette since our phone call began and was only now giving in. "What if he doesn't want to be found? What if he doesn't want to see you?"

"Charlie, this is *Pierce* we're talking about."

"Honey, it's not the same guy. I mean—even if it is the same guy, it's not. You know what I mean?"

"Yes. So what?"

"I think you should forget it, that's what."

"I can't forget it."

~

We stayed with my parents until New Year's Day. After the phone call to Charlie, I felt better—purged, maybe. It helps to articulate something. And Charlie, despite his reservations, hadn't thought I was entirely crazy. And hearing Charlie's voice—well, it was good to hear his voice. His voice hadn't changed over the years. Hearing it reminded me of things, and if I were going to track down Pierce I needed to be reminded. I had lost him, he had died for me at least twice, three times, how many times, but I would go in search of lost time, *à la recherche de temps perdu,* and I would find him again.

On New Year's Eve, James and I skated on the pond just before dark. He was feeling romantic: we waltzed, and he kissed me when we got around the willow tree to the part of the pond my mother couldn't see from the window. I leaned against him, balancing against his big chest. I had given him a bright red cashmere muffler for Christmas, and I felt it soft against my cheek.

"You've been in a funny mood," he said.

"It's been this thing with Denis," I said. "This Yale thing." It wasn't a lie. I had talked it over with my mother, who was ecstatic— she missed her only grandchild—and her happiness had, for some reason, made me think that the whole idea was too good to be true. Denis's Christmas card had said, "See you soon, I fondly hope!"

I told my mother my fears—my belief that any dealings I had with Emile were fated to end in disaster. "My disaster," I said.

"Christine, you've been divorced from that dreadful little man for twelve years." My mother had gradually come to find the idea of Emile ludicrous. She always called him "that dreadful little man" even though he was over six feet tall. In her mind, he was a carica- ture—the shrimpy, scheming Frenchman with the goatee. She even refused to like *Lucy's Pup.* She said she'd read that plot a million times, from *Bunny Blue* to *Lassie Come Home.* "He's not trying to torment you any more. He can't be such a monster."

"Oh, really?"

"Even monsters have to mellow over the years," my mother said. "Look at the Loch Ness Monster—they've made a cartoon show out of him."

Out on the pond, James took my cold hands and said, "But you want Denis to come?"

"Yes. I'm just scared."

"I really think it'll be okay," he said. "He's a good steady kid, and he loves you. You know that."

"He loves me now, James. Or he seems to. How do I know what his real feelings are? And how much will he love me when we're in the same town, when I'm a reality instead of some kind of abstract idea of Mom?"

"You won't see him that much. He'll live at Yale."

I smiled at him. "Am I supposed to hope I don't see much of my son when he gets here so that he won't start hating me?"

"You know I don't mean that," said James. "And how could anyone hate you, anyway? Give me a break."

We had champagne with dinner (my mother's pork roast with sauerkraut, a New Year's Eve tradition) and an apple tart made by James. My mother and James and I played Scrabble, and my father fell asleep in his chair with Ruby on his lap. James shook him awake at midnight, doing his duty, and said, "Happy New Year, Pop," and in his confusion my father said, "Happy New Year to you, Robbie, my boy. And many more."

⌒⌒⌒ *Chapter Five*

It was all very slow. The smallest thing in my search for Pierce
seemed to take a long time. Just to find Haver & Schmidt: when James
and I got back from my parents' place, I called Information in Stamford and there was no listing. It took me a week to recover from this
tiny setback, a week during which I drifted in a sort of coma of despair, questioning everything, from the wisdom of my search to the
validity of my existence.

When I snapped out of it, I tried Information in Manhattan, which
with agitating speed gave me a number for Haver & Schmidt. I was so
unnerved by the victory that I missed the number twice and had to
call back so the disembodied robot-voice could tell it to me again.

After that—the first evidence that I hadn't dreamed everything, or
been temporarily insane—I froze again, but it wasn't with despair or
hopelessness. On the contrary, I was in the grip of an ecstatic, manic
excitement that frightened me and that I knew I had to eliminate if
I was going to succeed at my task. Sometimes, when I thought of
what I was about to do, my hands grew clammy and my heart beat
fast, and I would get my Pierce collection down from the closet shelf
to stare at the photographs, leaf through the old playbills (Pierce as
Horatio, Pierce as Henry, Pierce as the has-been movie star in *Dinner
at Eight*), browse in the book of Van Gogh's letters to his brother, until the sense of Pierce's presence in those objects would become real to
me. I would breathe more easily then and be able to put it all away,

return to my painting or cook dinner like a normal person and not like someone on the verge of madness. In this way, wasting time, I gradually got used to the idea that my search for Pierce was real and possible, and I composed myself for it.

Another, more practical thing kept me from action. I had the phone number of Haver & Schmidt—that had been my first, irrevocable step—but I hadn't thought about what I would say to Alison Kaye. The more I did, at last, ponder that question, the more paralyzed I felt. I could think of nothing plausible. The truth, which had been convincing and even impressive when I told it to Charlie, seemed trumped-up when I imagined confessing it to Alison Kaye. *I sat next to you on the train last October, I spied on you, I knew someone named Orin Pierce, I thought he was dead, how can I reach him.*

I am not a natural liar: I lack the proper quick, inventive imagination. (Pierce, I thought—how Pierce could carry this off!) Worst of all, I had no one to consult: if I'd been able to try out my scenarios on, say, James, my task would have been easier. But I spent a lot of energy keeping James from perceiving my state of mind.

That state of mind involved the obsessive improvisation of fully-imagined other worlds. Wherever I went, whatever I was doing, I was also making phone calls, I was going to New York, I was talking with Alison Kaye, I was confronting Pierce. I think I must have been like a poet, who goes about her daily life while all the while a poem grows in her head. Or a playwright, except that, in this particular drama, half the dialogue would be ad-libbed and beyond my control. Or like an explorer in a strange land pursuing some elusive and possibly nonexistent goal, seeking a New World where there might be savages, there might be wild animals, there might be gold. I pictured the loneliness of that quest, and it was my own loneliness during that strange winter, while I lived my domestic life painting bowls of oranges and talking to James and sitting by the fireplace with a book and a cat on my lap, talking all the while to the people in my head. It seemed to me that poets, writers, explorers—anyone propelled by a vision of a more perfect world—must be sublimely happy souls.

January, then February. We had a blizzard, a thaw, a spell of springy weather, and James baked me a heart-shaped white clam pizza for Valentine's Day. Not long after that I was standing by the window watching Ruby rolling on her back in a patch of sun by the garage. There were the beginnings of buds on the forsythia; the witch hazel was in yellow bloom. Every day the sun was higher in the sky, and darkness came later. I thought: soon it will be spring. My birthday was coming. Denis would be hearing from Yale. George would be calling me about the show I was supposed to be getting ready for.

Standing there with the sun moving across the yard toward my window, I felt gripped by urgency. Before I could think any more I went to the front-hall phone, dialed the number of Haver & Schmidt in New York, and asked for Alison Kaye.

The receptionist said, "Whom may I say is calling?"—the *whom* pronounced very distinctly. Whom, indeed? I had considered using a pseudonym—Christine Laurent, perhaps, the name I had repudiated years ago when Emile and I were divorced. (I had always disliked it, it felt foreign to me, and pronouncing it the proper French way— gargling the r and trailing it off into a nasal ambiguity—was awkward.) But I decided that a false name would complicate things. I didn't want complications.

"Christine Ward," I said, and waited.

I waited and I stayed calm. In those few moments, I learned something about myself: that I could be calm, I could hold my own, I could function in a stressful situation. This hadn't been true ten, twelve years ago. Somewhere, I had picked up the ability to live in the world—to cope. Dr. Dalziel used to talk about *coping strategies*. Here is a coping strategy, Dr. Dalziel: Resurrect the dead. I smiled at my face in the hall mirror and waited, impatiently, to see what lies I would tell.

"This is Alison Kaye." Her voice was rushed and impatient, exactly what I had expected.

"Ah—yes—this is Christine Ward," I said, fixed on my reflection in the mirror as if I were watching myself on television. "You may not remember me, but we met at a party last fall." The party had come to me just a few days before, while I was absently opening and closing the black-and-gold matchbook from Tynan's—that dear, dead New Haven pub where Pierce and I hung out when I used to take the train up to New Haven to try to persuade him he should give graduate school another try. "I was with Andy Morgan—I don't know if you even remember him—but Orin Pierce was at the same party—?" I ended on a vague, interrogatory lift, keeping my voice brisk, never hesitating.

"Oh God." She gave a little bark of a laugh. "That awful Deaver Fairchild cocktail party? What a mad scene, and it was at least 95 degrees in there."

"Right," I said. On my yellow pad, I wrote: *Deaver Fairchild.* "So you do remember me?"

"Not really, but it had to be that party because I know Orin was there. Along with everybody else on earth." She seemed to relax, to sit back in her chair and welcome this short break from whatever she did at Haver & Schmidt. "What was your name again? Sorry."

"Christine Ward," I said, and paused very briefly before I added, "The painter."

"Oh, of course."

I smiled again into the mirror. *Pierce, you would be proud of me.* I went on, "What I'm calling for, Alison, is to ask you about Orin. I don't really know how to get in touch with him. He gave me a phone number and I scribbled it on a cocktail napkin or something, Lord knows, and I can't find it. I don't even know who he's with now."

"Well, no wonder. That guy has been moving around more than Eberhard Emmett, if you know what I mean." She laughed, and I snorted my own knowing little laugh in reply. "Right now he's with Parker, at least as far as I know." I wrote it down—*Parker*—at the top of my yellow page. Alison said, "Wait a minute, I've got the number here somewhere." I heard her rummaging, while she made a musical, temporizing sound (hmm, hmm, hmm) and I stared at *Parker.* Beside it I wrote *Eberhard Emmett.* "Are you looking to buy or sell?" she asked me.

"Oh—to buy," I said. "At the moment, I'm in Connecticut," I added—an irrelevancy imparted out of an urge toward some kind of honesty.

"I see," she said, which surprised me. What could she possibly see from that statement? "Well, he's got some beauties."

"Great." Before I could puzzle that out, she said, "Ah, here we go. Got a pencil?" She gave me a phone number and an extension. I tried to think of a way to ask her what kind of outfit Parker was, what Pierce was selling, what these "beauties" were, but even my new, confident liar's persona could come up with nothing.

"I really appreciate this," was all I could say. This was true: I was ashamed of spying on her on the train, of speculating about her sex life, of lying so outrageously and using her. She didn't even sound like some stereotypical cold-hearted yuppie; she sounded quite nice. *I will be grateful to you until I die, Alison Kaye.*

"Give him a call," she said. "If he can't help you, he'll know who can." Art? Antiques? Yachts? Drugs? "Let me warn you, though— how well do you know Orin?"

"Not very well, actually," I said. "I haven't really seen him in ages."

"Well, he's a real con artist," Alison said, with her biggest chuckle so far. "I'm not saying he's not a sweetheart, but keep a cool head. And give me a call one of these days—we'll do lunch."

~

Pierce sent me the postcard of Van Gogh's "The Night Café" soon after he got to New Haven, where he would spend exactly one semester studying at the Yale School of Drama before he dropped out. "The Night Café" was one of Pierce's favorites; when anyone asked him why he had come to Yale, he replied that he wanted to be near "The Night Café." (It was a mean little test he set people: would they know what he was talking about or not?) The first time I came to visit him, he took me to the Yale Art Gallery to look at the painting, and he quoted to me what Van Gogh had said of it, something about trying to express the most terrible passions of humanity by means of red and green.

I used to study the postcard, and go periodically to look at the painting, trying to understand what Van Gogh had meant. I never got it. To me, the painting looked bleak in spite of its color: the red and green café seemed merely sad, the people in it drunk or desperate or consumed with anomie, the hanging lamps lighting what should have been dimmed or in shadow. But I saw no human passions; in that café, all passion seemed spent.

When I said this to Pierce, he said to me, "The trouble is probably that you lack passion, Chris." I had unthinkingly accepted that comment as truth, as one of my store of major insights, and it had haunted me for years. It continued to haunt me, but I was no longer positive that it was valid. I got out Pierce's postcard ("We could really liven this place up!" he had scrawled on the back) and tacked it on the wall over the kitchen sink where I could look at it every day. I still didn't see in the painting the claim Van Gogh had made for it, but what I was feeling surely—surely—had everything to do with passion.

~

I dialed the number Alison had given me, and the receptionist said, "Parker Properties."

"Is this the investment company?" I asked. A stockbroker seemed the most incongruous profession I could concoct for this new Pierce, this businessman who had risen from the ashes of the Pierce who used to sit on the floor and play the guitar and believe what the Beatles said, that money can't buy you love. But I had fixed on the idea that Orin Pierce's "beauties" were stocks and bonds, and I had seen myself approaching him with imaginary money to invest.

"This is Parker Properties," the receptionist said patiently. "This is a real estate brokerage."

"Ah, of course," I said, and asked for extension 667. It occurred to me that I should hang up and think for a while. I should reorient myself from stocks and bonds to condos and interest rates. But I wanted to get on with it, I wanted something to happen. For twenty years, it seemed to me, I had been waiting for this moment: for Pierce to return to me.

"Yes," a voice said.

"Is this Orin Pierce?"

"Yes, it is."

He didn't sound like Pierce; he sounded like some man in an office in New York.

"Hello? Is there something I can do for you?"

I took a deep breath. It was too soon for conclusions, certainly too soon for disappointment. And the neutral voice, I realized, helped me to stay in control. If he had sounded exactly like Pierce as I remembered him—a voice I couldn't hear in my head, that I could recall only as being warm, intimate, the voice of a dear friend—I don't know what I would have done. I said, "I was given your name by Alison Kaye. She said you'd be a good person to talk to."

"Well, I hope that's true. What exactly are you interested in?"

"I'm thinking about buying. Sort of. I mean, I haven't made up my mind."

"Would you like to come in and we'll talk about it? Tell me what you need, and I'll show you some things. Were you thinking of the city, or what? Most of what I handle is right here in Manhattan—I'm sure Alison told you that. You're thinking of a condo, I assume. This is for yourself? Your family? Or what?"

Desperately, in the spaces between his words, I tried to bring back Pierce's voice. It had been clear and pleasant and expressive—an actor's voice—but not startlingly individual. He had had no particular accent: born in Connecticut, but his parents were university professors who lived all over the place before they settled down to tenure at Yale. I tried to remember quirks of diction, of inflection. I tried to bring back his singing voice—it was deeper than Charlie's, with a slight bluesy roughness he could put on at will. I could remember what I could only call the *feel* of it, the sensation of being in his presence when he spoke, or of watching him onstage—as Horatio, say, in doublet and tights, or as Henry in *Becket* wearing some kind of velvet robe we used to kid him about. But I could remember nothing specific: where his voice had been there was nothing but silence.

Could this have been Pierce? It could have been anyone.

"Just myself," I said. "I'm living in Connecticut right now, but I'm a painter, and I'd like to relocate to Manhattan. At least I think I would. I'm kind of toying with the idea."

I waited for him to say: Ah, Connecticut, yes, I'm from New Haven, my parents were at Yale, I even went to grad school there for a while, the Drama School, I know Connecticut well. "You want to be closer to the action—the museums and the galleries, the art scene."

"Yes—I suppose I do."

"And will this be your studio as well as your residence?"

"Yes." I answered mechanically, listening to him. Would Pierce say *the art scene,* would he say *close to the action?* Everything Pierce used to say was tinged with irony; he couldn't have said *the art scene* without putting it in quotes. But that was twenty years ago. I wished I had a photograph of Pierce in front of me, to try to match the voice to the face. "Yes, I prefer to work at home," I said.

"And so you'll need plenty of room to spread out, I would guess— a spare bedroom, maybe, with good light."

"Yes, yes, that would be great, the light is the main thing. And a view, that would be lovely."

"Well." He cleared his throat. I felt desperate: all I wanted was to hang up. I couldn't bring Pierce to my mind at all; every minute, I was losing him more. He had been superseded by the humorless man who went with the voice on the phone, the boringly ingratiating manner, the professional vocabulary: I saw a man with over-styled hair and an ostentatious silk tie, a tan from a tanning parlor, muscles from a gym. If someone like Pierce had wanted to disappear, he had found a perfect disguise.

He said, "I think I can do something for you. Of course, a lot is going to depend on what price range you're talking. But we can get to that when you come in. I'm sorry—what did you say your name was?"

This part, at least, I had planned. I couldn't give the name Pierce had known until I had seen this man: what if he did reject me? What if he heard my name and hung up on me? "Louise Laurent," I said, pronouncing it the Anglo way that Emile hated.

He spelled it and asked, "Are you French?"

"Oh no," I said. "that's my ex-husband's name," and immediately wished I hadn't said it. I wanted my own disguise: the less this Pierce knew about me, the less he would want to flee. This man was not Pierce. But if he were: if somehow, in his long secret life, he had heard about my marriage to the well-known illustrator, Emile Laurent... "My husband Pierre was Canadian, actually," I said. "I'm a widow."

"I see. Well. Louise. Shall we set up an appointment? I'm afraid this week is out, but next week looks good, except possibly Tues-day—"

We made a date, and I hung up. I felt nothing but confusion, and something close to despair. Whatever happened could not be good— could not satisfy me—and yet I had to know whatever was there to be known. I went to the closet and took down the picnic basket and looked at the photographs of Pierce. I hadn't liked this man on the phone: I didn't want him to be Pierce. And yet I did want him to be Pierce. I wanted Pierce, at any price—ugly ties, salesman's jargon, fake tan. And of course my impression could be all wrong: his phone manner was something he had developed because it sold condos, he would hang up the phone and get his guitar from a closet, he would throw off his expensive jacket and play along with his old Big Bill Broonzy records. Or the whole thing could be part of his costume, the stage set he had placed himself in for reasons of his own. A real estate broker: how bizarre, how unlikely, how perfect.

The photographs, as usual, told me nothing. I closed my eyes and tried to listen. *The trouble is that you lack passion. Will no one rid me of this turbulent Charles. The last poor oryx, I knew him, Horatio.* On impulse, I hunted up an old Everly Brothers record—a relic from James's high school days in Baltimore:

Whenever I want you
All I have to do is dream . . .

If only that were true, I thought. The song brought back those happy evenings in Pierce's room. Unexpectedly, it brought back making love with Charlie. It brought back the sensation of huddling against a wind that swept across a flat landscape—the hard Ohio winters and reluctant springs. It did not bring back Pierce.

I should have listened to Proust, to Marcel in *Swann's Way*. We have our memories, but they're like the photographs of Pierce that I had hoarded: my responses to them were comfortable, learned, ritualized. They told me nothing new. The true nature of the past is hidden, outside the realm of effort, or imagination, or intellect. The past offers itself back to us only by chance, when we aren't looking for it—like a lost earring under the radiator, whose gleam we glimpse from across the room when we've given up looking and are occupied with something else. The past emerges in a cup of tea, a madeleine, a tree—a skull in a fifteenth-century painting. I should have known I wouldn't find what I was looking for, that I would have to wait until it found me.

The voice on the phone could have been Pierce's. It could have been anyone's. But the important thing was that it could have been

Pierce's, and I was foolish enough to believe that in six days I would know the truth.

~

I lived in a city for the sake of James, who said he needed people, rooftops, pollution, traffic jams, or he'd go mad. I still preferred small towns with farmland close by, like the area where I grew up, or the flatlands of northern Ohio, and if there were any real countryside around New Haven I would have agitated for a move there. But the southern Connecticut countryside was mostly suburban, or becoming suburban, or self-consciously over-countrified, and in every case too expensive for James and me.

But I had become fond of New Haven. I loved our little Bishop Street house and its slowly gentrifying neighborhood. I had developed a real love for walking in the city, though the mix of neighborhoods within its tiny confines could be frightening. I never walked near the Hill section, where every day it seemed someone was shot, or into the streets between Dixwell Avenue and the gun factory, where James used to work with troubled teenagers. And I never walked west, out to my old neighborhood where I had lived so miserably after Emile left me and before I met James.

The weather became prematurely springlike, and, after my talk with the Orin Pierce of Parker Properties, I began taking long walks in the afternoons—my reward for a morning spent working on the books for Jimmy Luigi's or trying to paint. The air was warm and wet, and the browns and greys of the sidewalks gleamed in the fitful rays of sunshine that emerged every day just before it began to get dark. I used to walk out Orange Street, past the markets and the pretty old churches and the building where Pierce used to live (a gloomy stone pile that has since been turned into condos), and end up at the park. I marched up and down the path with my hands stuffed in the pockets of my old plaid jacket, watching elderly ladies walking their dogs, and groups of nursery school kids who ran for the swings every mild afternoon. I felt I could watch these people for hours. Or I'd walk the other way, up to Whitney Avenue, and down to the Green and up Chapel Street. Sometimes I'd stop in and say hello to James and Raymond, but often I would just keep going, as far as the

British Art Center, where I liked to sit in the library and read English periodicals, or over to the Yale Art Gallery, where I would stop in and stare compulsively at "The Night Café." Then I would have a cup of tea at Atticus or Willoughby's, and—thinking of Denis—watch the students with their spiked hair or their preppy sweaters or any variation in between.

I didn't allow Pierce into my mind at all. Even standing in front of the Van Gogh, I didn't let myself think of Pierce. I puzzled over the bleak yellow light from the starry lamps, and the clock whose hands didn't work together properly to register the time. (Was it 12:15 or 1:15? Neither seemed quite right.) But I didn't think of Pierce—not because I was taking the advice of Proust and letting the past lie until it leapt out at me, but because the idea of Pierce exhausted and disturbed me. I wasn't even sure how to think of Pierce any more. For a long time, through all the vicissitudes of my life, I had been able to take a certain comfort from the thought of him. Now there was only confusion and anxiety. It was mad to believe he was alive, sitting in an office building, answering extension 667 when it rang, talking price ranges and number of bedrooms: that Pierce was unreal and impossible. But so was Pierce dead and crumbled to dust in his grave—the last poor oryx. What would I think if I let my mind settle on Pierce? My beloved friend was dead, even if he wasn't dead. And of course he was. But either way, he didn't bear thinking of.

I walked the criss-cross paths of the New Haven Green. Occasionally, there was a musician, a hot-dog stand, a balloon vendor. Teenagers carried huge blasting radios on their shoulders. There were construction noises from the old town hall and the library. Pigeons scattered when I approached them, then regrouped, their wings making papery sounds. People asked me for money—mostly young black men and old white women—and sometimes I gave them a quarter or two and sometimes I just shook my head. I walked briskly, thinking about what to cook for dinner, noticing the way the late afternoon sunlight turned the wet brown sidewalks to bronze. If I met someone I knew, I stopped to talk about the wonderful weather, the progress on town hall, the news. Sometimes I stopped to buy a magazine or some cookies. And then I would come to my narrow blue house, where the cats, just waking up, would hear my key in the lock and come to meet me, and James would come in soon after, and we would work in the kitchen, and have dinner, and talk or read or go to a movie or walk down to Christopher Martin's for a beer, and I would fall asleep worn out.

In this way I crossed off the days.

~~~ *Chapter Six*

My appointment with Orin Pierce was for four o'clock. His office turned out to be on the sixty-sixth floor of a new building in midtown Manhattan. It was ridiculously, tastefully palatial—hardly what I expected: antique tables, brass lamps, mellow old oil paintings. I was wearing an ancient black wool turtleneck with paint on the sleeve, and jeans tucked into my rubber lace-up boots. (Silvie had bought me the boots in Paris years ago. I had a letter from Denis: "*Grand'-mère* Silvie is bringing you home some boots. She knows you do not wear boots of animals, so these are strange boots of rubber, up to the knee, with laces.") I gave my name, feeling like someone who had come to solicit contributions for a home for aging hippies.

The elegant, unflappable receptionist said, "Mr. Pierce is expecting you, have a seat." I sat for a few minutes in a tufted leather chair the color of fine sherry, ostensibly looking at a pile of real-estate prospectuses (deluxe high-rise apartments with identical skyline views like paintings on velvet) but really wishing I hadn't come, and then I was shown into his office.

He rose to greet me. "Ah! Ms. Laurent," he said, and I was stunned into silence. My first thought was *yes,* followed immediately by *no,* and then I gave up and stood there confused, staring at him. He gave me no sign of recognition. I had never remembered to wonder how much I had changed in twenty years—not so much, I thought. Not so much as this man. Because if he was Pierce, he had changed from a lean young man with thick brown hair that fell in his eyes, to a heavy-set, bearded, balding man with creases across his forehead. The kind of man who wore a three-piece suit, a watch chain stretched across his vest, rimless glasses which he was polishing with a silk paisley handkerchief.

He put his glasses back on and shook my hand; his hand told me nothing: it was warm and dry, the handshake was firm. "How extremely nice to meet you," he said.

It was indeed if he were in disguise or in costume—playing a kindly visiting uncle in a Merchant-Ivory movie or the White Rabbit in *Alice in Wonderland*. I couldn't speak. After the first shock, I could barely look at him—the smile, the brown beard. I looked beyond him to the window and the view from the sixty-sixth floor: immense sky, a glance down to puddled rooftops, the river sparkling in the distance, and at eye level, coming our way, was a helicopter. All I could think was: after that plunge down the canyon, how can he bear this height? And realized the idiocy of that thought, the extent of my confusion. I immediately became dizzy, and had to hang on to the back of a chair.

"Are you all right?"

He stood beside me. I hung on. The helicopter began to descend. I watched the blur of its propeller until it slipped below us, out of sight. When I turned to meet his eyes, he was smiling. He said, "Here—sit down. The height often has that effect on people. Would you like a glass of water?"

"Please."

He poured from a glass carafe into a tumbler shot with gold. "There are times when we're actually above the clouds. Or sometimes it's snowing up here, with sun and blue skies down below. It's really amazing." I drank, staring at him, wanting to run out the door, with the feeling that everything had gone wrong—though I couldn't have said in what way I had expected it to go right. Was he supposed to cry, "Chris!" and sweep me up in a hug? Or be a seven-foot-tall stranger with coal-black hair, or be Pierce, definitely Pierce, but in the grip of amnesia, from which I would tenderly bring him back? Anything but this, all wrong—the alarming view, his impersonal kindness, his watch chain, his lightly-freckled bald head, his beard.

He was sitting across his desk from me, still smiling, though somewhat anxiously. "It does get to people sometimes. Would you like me to draw the curtains?"

"No, it's nothing, I'm fine now," I managed to say.

"It doesn't bother me at all," he said. "But some people just don't have a head for heights."

"Yes."

"They get sick, they get panicky." He shrugged, and his smile turned reassuring. "There's no hurry. Take your time."

I drained the glass, remembering the calm that filled me when I talked to Alison Kaye. I closed my eyes and breathed deeply. I opened my eyes. I didn't look toward the window. I looked at Orin Pierce. I said, "Well," and tried to smile back at him. "Tell me something about Manhattan real estate. I'm a real babe in the woods here, and I want to know what I'm getting into."

He immediately switched into a new gear. He told me about the frenzy of development in the city, about neighborhoods, about condominium fees and creative financing. I studied him, watching him talk—his mouth, his gestures, his eyes. I tried to figure out why my first reaction had been that this was Pierce, and why I had then decided it wasn't.

The *no* was easier: he was bearded, bald, aging. He was immaculately dressed—a bit of a dandy. He was also, in his way, handsomer than Pierce. His small hands looked manicured: could they have once held a guitar? a marijuana cigarette? a skull lifted from a biology lab? He was—I searched for a word—*unctuous?* Eager to please, at least.

Pierce was sarcastic. Pierce was scruffy. He was skinny, full of nervous energy. He cared nothing for clothes. But looking at this man, I realized that he had reminded me, in that first second, of Pierce's father, the history professor, whom I had met twice, and who had been bald in exactly the way this man was: bald as a monk, the tonsure bordered with thick brown hair as neatly trimmed as fringe on a curtain.

But that wasn't the only thing. There was something about him—indefinable, elusive, possibly deliberately held back, but definitely there—a hint of recklessness that recalled Pierce: a tone in his voice beneath the polite business talk, a look in his eyes, as if he had raced motorcycles in his youth, or been a big-time gambler. Or had, before he assumed this dual disguise of middle age and propriety, been Pierce. And looking at his dark blue eyes, I was able to remember that Pierce's eyes were blue.

He wound up his speech and looked at me expectantly. I had taken in almost nothing of what he said, and I wasn't sure what to do. Why go on with it? Why give him the story I had prepared, a naïve request for four rooms in a small, old-fashioned, friendly building close to a park? Why tell him the price range I had carefully worked out on the train coming down?

And yet I wasn't sure, I wasn't even remotely sure of anything. He and Pierce had blue eyes, he and Pierce's father had bald heads, he had a look in his eye that I fancied reminded me of Pierce. The fact remained that he hadn't recognized me. There hadn't been the smallest sign, not one. True, Pierce was an actor. But he had acted onstage, not in his life—had he? Not with me. In that moment, when I tried to decide what to say, Charlie's question hit me hard: if this was Pierce, why was he pretending to be a bald man in a three-piece suit who sold real estate? I wished Charlie were with me. I began to wonder if I could photograph him and send Charlie the result for his opinion.

He said, "It might help if you tell me exactly what you're looking for."

I looked into his eyes and knew I had to answer truthfully. There was nothing else I could do. I said, "I'm looking for you."

"I beg your pardon?"

In that instant I was sure: the irony was there, the crooked smile, the head held to one side, the narrowed eyes. (Yes, blue. How could I have forgotten that dark sea-blue?) And then—he frowned, he leaned forward to pour me another glass of water—it was gone. But not quite.

"Orin Pierce," I said, and drank.

"Do we know each other?"

I stared at him helplessly. His bald head gleamed. His beard and moustache matched his hair exactly: three versions of the same thick brown hedge. Behind his glasses, there were crow's feet around his eyes, pouches under them. Sadness filled my throat. "You don't recognize me?"

He gave a small laugh. "I wish I could say I did. I don't know anyone named Louise Laurent."

"Christine Ward," I said. "Pierce it's me—Chris." There was a flicker in his eyes—something. I leaned over and gripped his hand across the desk. "Pierce. Why are you doing this? It's me."

He smiled—a smile I would remember afterward not as Pierce's crooked, dubious one but as a smile full of pity. "My dear woman," he said. "I don't know you. I've never seen you before. I don't understand this. There's a mistake here somewhere."

The sadness overcame me. I began to cry.

He was very nice. He lent me his silk handkerchief and then, more practically, found a box of Kleenex in a drawer of his desk. He got a bottle of Scotch from a cupboard and poured me a shot. He drew the curtains—"This view isn't helping"—and patted my shoulder, saying, in a White Rabbit voice, "Oh dear, I wish I knew what this was all about."

I gave up. It was a grotesque coincidence, a cosmic joke. But it wasn't being played by Pierce, or by this man. I didn't know whom to blame it on except myself.

~

We went out for a drink. I was his last appointment for the day, he said. He wanted to hear about this other Orin Pierce. He was intrigued. He was sorry I didn't want to buy a piece of real estate, but he wanted to hear my story. There was a little bar around the corner, nice and quiet.

"I'm not dressed," I said. My clothes were bad enough; I imagined my face after my weeping fit.

"You're fine," he said. "You look lovely, really you do." He took off his glasses and smiled. "With or without my glasses." He stored the glasses carefully in a case, which he put into his desk. (Pierce would never be so neurotic, he would have lost the glasses ages ago and done without them.) He straightened the papers on his desk. Then he paused, looking at me, and asked, "It wasn't the view, then?"

I looked toward the window. "Oh—no, I don't think so."

"Then check it out," he said. "It's really magnificent."

He took my arm and steered me over, and New York lay below us again, sparkling. Orin Pierce and I stood by the window, looking down. As we watched, lights went on here and there. The late afternoon sky was brilliantly blue, rosy at the horizon with the beginning of sunset.

"It's very peaceful up here," he said. "Another world. Like being in heaven. There's the Queensboro Bridge. The roof of the IBM Building, a mere forty-two stories. And look at the flagpoles in Central Park." He touched my arm, close enough to me that I could feel his breath on my cheek. "Like toothpicks," he said.

I moved away, my heart beating fast. The shining miniature city frightened me, for that brief moment, in some elemental, nightmarish way, but not because of the height: it was because of Orin Pierce standing so close to me.

"I'm off for the day, Flo," he said to the receptionist as we left. He shrugged into a camelhair topcoat. He had a red scarf like the one I gave James. "I'm going to play a little hooky."

Flo looked up from her computer and said, "You might want to know that Mr. Greenwood called."

"Nope. Not interested." He winked at her, and she smiled back, demurely. "That's what I pay you for, babe. To protect me from guys like Greenwood."

She watched, pretending not to, as he helped me into my old black pea jacket.

"See you in the morning, Florence."

"See you in the morning, Mr. Pierce."

We walked around the corner to a bar called the Metro. He held my arm as we walked. "This place has saved my life a million times. There are days when I get out of work and I don't know what in hell I'm doing in this world and an hour in the Metro straightens me out. Don't ask me why I'm in this crazy business. It's not because I love it, that's for sure. Same thing goes for this city."

The Metro was nearly deserted. There was a sweep of mahogany bar with a brass rail, and high-backed booths under Tiffany lamps. I imagined him coming in here after work, drinking too much, then going home to watch television alone in a deluxe condominium like the ones in the Parker brochures. I thought of my postcard of "The Night Café" tacked over the sink, and it seemed improbable to me that Orin Pierce needed a refuge like this.

We took a booth in a far corner, and he smiled at me. "So," he said. "Was it true that you're a painter?"

"Yes."

"And you're the widow of a Canadian named Laurent?"

"No. He's French, and we're divorced."

"And you live in Connecticut?"

"Yes." I studied his face. "Pierce was from Connecticut."

He laughed. "It's so weird that you call this guy Pierce. You say his name was Orin, like mine."

"He never liked it."

"It brings back my schooldays. Beer okay?" A waiter came, and he ordered Australian lager for both of us. "In my prep school, it was last names only. I went to prep school in Connecticut, as a matter of fact."

"Oh? Where?" I had that sudden dropping feeling in my stomach. I had one of my quick, desperate fantasies of amnesia, of myself putting together clues for him, piecing his life back together, helping him rise from the dead: I would be his cup of tea, his madeleine. I would free him from the prison of death.

He hesitated a moment, then said, "I went to St. Paul's." Why had he hesitated? What did it mean? In my heart, I knew it meant nothing. But I thought: I can verify this, I can check their records. He said, "Did I just fail some sort of test?"

"Pierce went to Hotchkiss."

"I'm sorry."

"Oh, this is absurd!" I leaned my cheek against the side of the booth. What were we talking about? My head began to ache.

He asked me, "This guy disappeared, or what?"

I said, "Yes, in a way." I felt like laughing, crying. I felt like getting out of there. I said, "This is so completely stupid. I should go."

"Wait," he said. "Wait. I graduated in '60." I just shook my head. "Come on. What about your friend?"

"I don't know," I said. "Pierce was '61, I guess. Same as me."

"What about you? Where did you go to school?"

"It hardly matters. Jamesville High School, Jamesville, New

York."

"Nice country up there," he said.

Was this irony? Was this some kind of torture? I thought of Pierce and Robbie playing catch in the driveway. The three of us down at the pond skipping stones. Pierce steering the cartful of clean laundry from unit to unit. Pierce and Robbie touching up the WARD'S SUNSET MOTEL sign. Then the drunken drive to Maine.

And Pierce: Pierce on the island with a gun in his hand.

"You know Jamesville?" I asked him.

"Driven through. I have friends in Rochester." The waiter brought the beer. Orin Pierce poured for us both, and raised his glass. I remembered his breath on my cheek, the smell of his skin (did I remember that?) when he stood beside me at the window. He was just my height—Pierce's height: tall for a woman, average in a man.

"To this weird conversation," he said, raising his beer glass. He drank, and smiled at me. I had a vague memory that Pierce's teeth were yellowish, crooked on the bottom. This man's teeth were white and even. Not that that meant anything. Dr. Mankoff once said of a patient, "We can't do anything about her face, but the good news is that we can totally reconstruct her mouth." New teeth, beard, moustache, bald head (shaved?), twenty pounds or so, twenty years . . .

I wanted to ask: Have you ever been to Maine? Do you have an old photograph of yourself?

He said, "We're getting off the subject. This Pierce guy. You know, he and I could easily have known each other. I played ice hockey. We used to play Hotchkiss all the time. I knew a lot of guys over there."

"But no Orin Pierce."

He shook his head. "The only Orin Pierce I've ever known is myself."

"But Pierce must have seen you play, he must have been aware that you had the same name."

He said, "He may have known me, but I sure didn't know him." He took a sip of beer. "This is pretty strange, if you ask me. If this were a movie, your Orin Pierce would have killed me and assumed my identity."

I looked at him: eyes, beard, bald head gleaming. "What would be his motivation?"

"If this were a movie?" He shrugged. "He's done some dastardly deed, and he wants to hide. He was a Weatherman in the sixties, blew up labs where they made napalm, killed someone by accident. He's a spy, a double agent, and someone's on his trail. You know how it goes." He took another sip of beer.

"But why use his own name? It doesn't make sense."

"It might. Hey—this is a movie." He grinned. "Don't walk out in the middle. Stay and see the end. Though I must admit it's an odd plot twist." He stared into space, thinking. "It's intriguing, though. Maybe he murdered someone. Or drove someone to his death."

Pierce with a gun in his hand, looking off into the amazing sunset.

"Christine? I'm sorry. I was kidding, I got carried away. Jesus, this is real life—not a movie. I'm sorry, I know this is important to you—whatever it is. I don't mean to make light of it. Are you all right?"

"Yes, I'm all right."

I excused myself and went to the women's room. In the mirror, my face was pale, all the blusher had worn off. My freckles stood out, and my hair looked very dark. I tried to assess what I saw: how much had I changed? My hair was only slightly gray. I had worn it long and braided in college. Then I'd had it cut very short, not so different from the way it was now. Pierce had known me both ways. I remembered the time I ran into Nancy Doyle, my fifth-grade pal, at Rockefeller Center. We hadn't seen each other since we were eleven, but I had known her instantly, she had known me . . .

I stared at myself: how could he not recognize me? The answer, of course, was: *he isn't Pierce.* But it was too strange—everything was too strange to be either untrue or coincidence. It was as if we had moved to another plane of existence, where there was truth, there was falsehood, and there was something else, a different kind of reality that included both.

I put on blusher, and peed, and ran cold water on my wrists, and took aspirin. When I returned to the table, I half expected him to be gone, but he was there, watching for me, his glass almost empty.

"Are you all right?"

"You keep asking me that," I said, smiling. I realized that I didn't dislike him: he was better, he was more human, in the cozy bar than in his skyscraper office. I could almost believe in his need to hit the Metro every day after work. Anyone can be lonely. I was reminded of when I used to go to Jimmy Luigi's for my pizza and beer. "I guess the answer is no, I'm not all right."

"You're troubled. This Pierce thing." He signaled to the waiter, a V with his fingers—two more beers. "Why don't you tell me about him? Who is this guy—this alter ego of mine?"

~

We stayed at the Metro drinking beer until after seven o'clock. I told him everything, from my first semester at Oberlin, to the night Charlie came up my back stairs and wept at my kitchen table, to the events of that day in New York.

I kept thinking I was finished, and then something else would strike me, something I'd forgotten. I told him about the Everly Brothers, the skull, Pierce's bald father, his old Volkswagen, the time he played Horatio, about Pierce's apartment in New Haven, "The Night Café," Charlie's Christmas card. I told him about Alison's Filo-Fax, the painting of St. Francis at the Frick. I told him about the photographs of Pierce that I kept in the old picnic basket. I told him the plot of *Swann's Way*. I even told him about the wind-up penguin and the sunset and the whole Plover Island incident—things I had never told anyone, things even Charlie didn't know.

He was, to say the least, a good listener, and talking was an enormous relief, but at the same time I felt ashamed, though I wasn't sure why—and disloyal, though I couldn't have said to whom. Pierce, probably: I was spilling the story of his life to someone he would dislike. But also James, who was happily ignorant of my madness, who thought I was seeing the *Anything Goes* revival with Silvie. And maybe myself: why was I telling my secrets to this man who was nothing to me?

But I went on talking. It was like talking to a bartender, or your seatmate on a plane: the queer, distanced quality was what made it easy and almost natural. I couldn't talk to James, and there were things I couldn't let Charlie in on, or anyone else, but I could tell everything to this familiar stranger. He listened quietly, saying little, nodding occasionally. He gave me his complete attention, as if his life depended on what I was saying. Or as if I were telling him the story of his own life. I talked until I couldn't talk any more, and when I was done, there was silence between us for a moment. He was probably waiting for me to continue. I said, "That's all," drank a long swallow of beer, and began to cry.

"You were crazy about this guy," Orin said.

I fumbled in my pocket for a tissue. "I suppose that's obvious."

"Very," he said. He added, "I'm sorry, Christine."

"You don't really have anything to apologize for," I said.

"I'm sorry I'm not Pierce." He picked up his empty glass and stared into it. "I'm sorry about that for a lot of reasons but one of them has nothing to do with you. I'm sorry nobody ever loved me that much." He sat down the glass and looked at me. "And I'm sorry he went and died on you."

The Metro was filling up. The bar at the front was three-deep in businessmen who dangled their briefcases in one hand and drank with the other. Several of them called hello to Orin, or waved, and stared at me. Someone stopped on his way to the men's room and said, "Mind if Mitch and I join you?"

Orin said, "Sorry, Jack, we're just leaving." He didn't introduce me. He looked at his watch and said, "Let's get out of here. Let's go out and have some dinner. This place is too noisy." I started to get up, but he gripped my hands suddenly and said, "Christine. I want to prove it to you. I want you to ask me questions so I can prove to you that I'm not the other Orin Pierce."

I looked at him blankly. "What questions? I don't know what to ask you."

"Ask me if I've ever been to New Mexico," he said. "If I ever lent my car, complete with driver's license, to a man who looked like me. If I decided to go into hiding for no good reason, assume a new identity but use my old name, let you and everyone else I ever knew—including my parents—think I died a gruesome death. Ask me that."

We stared at each other across the table. In the dim light, his eyes were restless and haunted, the way I remembered Pierce's eyes. "It sounds horrible," I said. "It sounds like someone horrible."

"It's not me, Christine." His hands still gripped mine, and I tried to pull them away, but he held on. "Do you believe me? That none of this happened? That I'm not him?"

I tried to make him smile. "I must admit I'm having serious doubts about it."

He let go my hands and forced a smile—not Pierce's. "Come on," he said. "Ever been to Clarissa's? Let's walk over there and get some food."

"I should make a phone call."

"Oh?"

I hadn't told him about James. I had told him about Pierce, I had talked about Pierce until I could hardly talk any more, but James seemed part of another world—the normal one, where truth was truth.

"I have to call a friend," I said.

"Call from Clarissa's."

When he helped me into my coat, his hands lingered on my shoulders. We were both slightly drunk. We walked by the bar; someone clapped him on the back and the man named Jack called out, "Hang in there, Orin."

Orin waved and steered me outside. The air was cold, and it sobered me up.

"Here—take this." He put his red scarf like James's around my neck and tucked it in. In the neon glow from the Metro sign, his face was, and wasn't, the face of Pierce. I knew that the longer I looked at him, the less I would see the Pierce I had known. He would be more lost to me than ever. It occurred to me that maybe that was a good thing.

"There is no satisfactory explanation for all this except coincidence," he said. "You know that. Your Pierce is gone, Christine. I'm not that guy."

"Maybe I just need to forget him. Maybe I was getting a little nutty on the subject."

"You can't mourn forever, babe."

I remembered the trees in my parents' back yard, the feel of the bark against my skin, Charlie crying in my arms. I wasn't sure that was true, but I said, "I suppose not."

We walked to Clarissa's—it was a seafood place—and ordered dinner and more Australian beer. We were silent for a while. I was exhausted. I was ready to believe Orin wasn't Pierce. I just didn't want to believe it. My eyes filled up again, and I dabbed them with my napkin.

"Chris?"

"Oh, God, it's difficult," I said. "I'm having a hard time, Orin."

I could see that he liked it that I called him by name. He touched his glass to mine and said, "I'm glad I met you. I want you to know that. I hope we can be friends." We drank, and he said, "But I want you to tell me the real problem."

"What real problem?"

"Your real problem with Pierce. You haven't told me everything. Come on. What's the deal? There's more to it, isn't there? Christine?"

I thought of the moment at the window, New York spread below us, sixty-six flights down, and I thought of Pierce's car sailing off into space. If this man was Pierce, what was he up to? And if he wasn't Pierce, why was he demanding this of me? If there was more to it, it was he who had the information.

"Who are you?" I asked him.

He pursed his lips, and a double furrow appeared between his eyebrows. *Will no one rid me of this turbulent Christine.* And then he did what Pierce used to do. He took my hand; he made his voice very gentle. I almost expected him to break into a chorus of *Bye Bye Love,* but he said, "You know who I am, Christine. I'm Orin Pierce. I have a co-op on East 57th Street. I'm 45 years old. I was born in Sarasota, Florida. I'm a real estate broker for Parker Properties. I've never laid eyes on you before in my life. I never heard of your friend Charlie. I did not go to Oberlin College, and I don't play the guitar. If you don't believe me, I can't help that. I walked into this thing as an innocent bystander, and I'm trying to help you out of it. Believe me," he said. "What you see is what you get."

I closed my eyes. I remembered Pierce as Henry in *Becket.* He got a standing ovation every night.

"We'll figure it out together, Christine. I know I'm not your old pal Pierce. You need to know it, too." With my eyes closed, his voice was different—unlike Pierce's voice as I thought I recalled it. Something in the accent. I opened my eyes. He raised my hand to his lips, kissed it, kept it there. I could get a photograph of Pierce's father, probably at Yale. I could call St. Paul's. I could check the birth records in Sarasota. "I don't want you to think badly of me," he said. "I don't want this to be between us. But it's important that we be honest with each other."

"I agree."

"So please, Christine. Just tell me."

In that instant, I was sure he was Pierce. The way he said my name, the half smile, the light in his eyes—I couldn't have explained it, but I was sure. And yet he couldn't be. "I think I'm going crazy," I said.

He kissed my hand again. "I can help. But you have to be honest with me."

I shook my head. "I need to forget this, Orin. I have nothing to say."

~

We ate lemon sole, talking carefully about neutral things: politics, I remember, and movies, painting, the various landmark preservation committees he was involved with—both of us conscious of the artificiality of our conversation, the studied impersonality of the topics we discussed. Several times, it occurred to me that he was deliberately cultivating me for some purpose I couldn't imagine: there was a quality of insincerity (very faint, like a foreign accent, or the lingering hoarseness from a cold) in everything he said, as if he really were an actor, a man who was neither Pierce nor Orin but someone impersonating both of them simultaneously.

While we were having coffee (Pierce used to drink his black, but Orin took cream), I remembered James. I hadn't called him, and I would have to hurry to catch the last plausible train. "You should just stay over," Orin said. He said it lightly, as if it were a matter-of-fact idea, the logical thing, but I had the idea that it was important to him, it gave him a kind of power over me. It was like the moment when we looked out of his window together, sixty-six stories down. "Stay with me," he said.

I flung down my napkin and pushed back my chair. "That's a ridiculous idea."

"Why not? Come on Christine, I'm not trying to—I mean, you

can sleep on the couch. It just makes sense."

I kept saying, "I just can't, I can't do that," while we put on our coats and Orin paid with a credit card. In some ways, of course, staying in New York did make sense. I hated going home on the late train—it was always slightly spooky, full of weirdos. And if I called now to say I was staying at Silvie's, James wouldn't worry. *James won't suspect anything,* was what I thought, and I disliked myself for it, and for not having told Orin about James. I hadn't forgotten my fleeting desire for George Drescher that fateful October day—his thumb caressing my palm. Was it true, what he had said? That there must be something wrong with my personal situation if I was imagining the past come to life? He had also said to let the dead rest in peace, don't dig them up.

Orin signed the receipt. His handwriting, I thought. I could compare it with Pierce's scrawl on the postcard. The idea seemed pointless, absurd. I would learn nothing: there was nothing to be learned. All of a sudden the only thing I wanted was to be home, by myself, so I could think.

"Ready?" Orin took my arm. "We'll have to run if you insist on catching that damned train."

"I've got to."

"Who's waiting for you?"

"It's complicated," was all I would say.

We ran the six blocks to Grand Central holding hands. At track sixteen, Orin said, "Of all the weird ways to meet a wonderful woman," and kissed me quickly. I pushed him away and got on the train, flopped into a seat and looked out the window. Orin was standing on the platform, searching for me. In that moment, before he caught my eye, he was nothing like Pierce, he was only himself—a handsome, bald, bearded man in a camel-hair coat and a bright red scarf, looking vulnerable and out of breath and somewhat lost. I still knew almost nothing about him: how he lived, who were the people in his life. He could be married, for all I knew. The lonely condo on East 57th could be filled with children, a dog, a wife cooking dinner, friends around a big table.

I remembered what he had said, about no one ever loving him the way I'd loved Pierce.

When he spotted me at the window, he raised his right hand, as if he were about to swear to tell the truth, the whole truth, and nothing but the truth. The train began to move. He smiled, and slowly, like a child, he waggled his fingers in a wave.

PART TWO

⌒ *Nightmare*

I feel that there is much to be said for the Celtic belief
that the souls of those whom we have lost are held captive
in some inferior being, in an animal, in a plant, in some
inanimate object, and so effectively lost to us until the
day . . . when we happen to pass by the tree or obtain
possession of the object which forms their prison.
Then they start and tremble, they call us by our name,
and as soon as we have recognized their voice the spell
is broken. We have delivered them: they have overcome
death and return to share our life.

Proust, *Swann's Way*

⌒~~~ *Chapter Seven*

My brother and I are sitting at a table under the trees. It is high summer, hot, but the trees provide an intermittent shade, and under them there is a breeze, or the illusion of a breeze: the patterns of the leaves move over the table top, across our hands, our teacups, and the plate of peanut butter cookies, so that things that are still seem to be ever so subtly in motion.

Peanut butter cookies are Robbie's favorite, and the teapot is his favorite teapot. When we were kids, my mother used to pour sweet, milky tea for us from that pot—a flowery thing, with buttercups painted on the side, trailing vines around the spout, and the lid trimmed with gilt. It belonged to my grandmother, who brought it with her from the west coast of Ireland. (She was from Sligo, where she worked in the family pub, The Four Winds, until she met my American grandfather and came to New York State as a bride.) Robbie was only three when she died, but I was eight, and I still have vivid memories of her soft accent: when I was very young, I asked my father, "Why does Gran sing when she talks?"—a cute moment from my babyhood that passed into the oral history of our family.

The teapot is nearly our only relic of Gran—that and two embroidered pillowcases that say "Good Morning" on one side and "Good Night" on the other. She never said why she went to the trouble of packing up just those objects and carrying them with her across the ocean in her little trunk. She was a practical woman, and there must have been a good reason, even if no one knows what it is. Robbie and I smile at each other, conscious of this teapot's history, and of ourselves as related, as part of a family, while we sit in the sun and pour our tea, his with plenty of sugar, mine with milk only.

It doesn't occur to either of us that the weather is too hot for tea—that icing it might be a good idea, that going to an air-conditioned place for a couple of beers might be even better. We're comfortable. We don't talk much. Being together again, with tea in Gran's old buttercup teapot, and the green shadows, and the pond shining blue out back—that's enough for the moment.

Robbie shot himself a few weeks before his twentieth birthday. Blew his brains out in the cabin in Maine. He had just finished his sophomore year at Dartmouth. I was five when he was born. He called me "Little Mommy." He was a big fat baby; I used to stuff him into his stroller and wheel him up and down the circular driveway in front of the motel office, singing to him. He liked only songs with animals in them: *How Much Is That Doggie in the Window?* and *Pop Goes the Weasel* and *The Cat Came Back* were his favorites. We shared a childhood and adolescence spent cleaning out motel bathtubs with Bab-O and loading hampers with dirty towels. We looked alike, with our mother's coloring and features: dark hair, pale skin, freckles, and a slight case of what my friend Bridget used to call an "overnose" (as opposed to an "undernose," which is what she has). In our parents' wedding picture, Mom looks like Robbie in drag. My son Denis resembles him so much it frightens me.

Robbie eats three cookies and has two cups of tea. I think, irrationally, that he must be starving, he hasn't eaten in so long. I try to correct myself, try to see this mad moment clearly, but my thoughts refuse to converge. There is a quick, blinding pain in my head, as if I were staring into the sun.

Robbie leans back in his chair and looks up at the sky and the moving treetops. He closes his eyes for a moment as if to tell me that his contentment is absolute, inexpressible, perfect, and must be fixed. Then he opens them, and we both look toward the pond.

"You're wondering why I'm here," he says.

"Yes." It's true that I have, urgently, wondered all this afternoon, but I have almost been hoping he wouldn't bring it up. I'm afraid of what he might say.

"There's something I've been wanting you to know," he says. "All this time."

It has been eight years, almost to the day. Not that I ever knew the day exactly, we just had an approximation by the coroner. But to the August day he was discovered.

"I want you to know it had nothing to do with Pierce, Chrissie," he goes on. "What happened. He wasn't involved. He sold me the .38, but that was months before I did it, when I met him that time in Boston. January or February, I can't remember. He really needed the dough, but I still had to practically twist his arm to get him to sell me the gun. And then I never saw him again. That's what I want you to know. If you think he was up in Maine with me, that he drove up to Plover Island before he went out West—" He lifts his hand and gestures toward the shining water, the trees, the bleached-out sky. "If you think we were fooling around with the gun again—forget it, Chrissie. He wasn't there. I swear it."

I stare at him until he turns his head and looks at me. It amazes me, how solid he looks—like a living person. I want to reach over and touch him, but I don't dare.

We sit there for a long time without saying another word, and I know that what he has told me is the truth.

"Then why did you do it?" I ask him at last.

He says, "I was depressed," and smiles slightly, as if to say: *what does it matter now?* I can tell that he has planned for my question and rehearsed this answer. The answer may be true, it may be false, but it's designed to make me shut up and drop the subject.

I can't bear it: all the old anguish returns. What does it matter now? To him, it matters not at all. To me—he's still my brother, still beloved, still missed. Still a puzzle.

"Depressed over what, Robbie, for Christ's sake?" It is the question I've wanted to shout at him for eight years. "How could you do it to us? Look at Dad, look at me—what you've put us through."

He turns back to the pond and gazes intently at its blueness. There could be tears in his eyes, I can't be sure.

"Robbie?"

"I'm sorry," he says, in a barely audible voice. "Forgive me. And believe what I told you," he adds. He looks me in the eye and his voice gets solemn—a kid's voice, swearing some ridiculous oath. Before my eyes, he gets younger, he is younger than Denis, he is fading away. He says, "About Pierce. I exonerate him. I hereby swear that he is innocent, and I formally exonerate him from all evildoing."

The shadows move across his face, and he's gone.

~

The first time Orin called, I said, "No. Please. I can't see you," and hung up. The second time, we talked for two hours. He had a knack for calling when James was out. The fourth time, I agreed to meet him in New York, at the Metro.

I told James I had to see George Drescher again.

James grinned at me and said, "Watch out for old George. I hear he's quite the boy."

~

I am trying to paint watercolor portraits of Pierce. I imagine him in Tynan's: yellows and browns. Or standing in the rain: blue and grey. I think of the colors of the Ohio landscape where we used to hike, and the amber, window-shade light of the New Haven apartment he shared with Charlie.

I can't get his face right. I can't remember his face. I can't paint. I can't do anything. Everything is wrong: the colors are too thin and wispy, too pastel, the brushwork is too tight.

If I am trying to express the terrible passions of humanity by means of yellow and grey and blue, I am not succeeding.

Emile says, "Maybe watercolor is not the best medium for what you're trying to do. Maybe you should be working in oil, or making charcoal sketches."

Emile is my painting teacher. I am taking a night class at the school where he teaches. In the daytime, I clerk in a bookstore. I am pitifully poor, but I want to work at my painting, and I know I need guidance.

"Of course, everything you do is exquisite," Emile says. "I just wonder if that's what you want for these subjects—that delicacy, that subtlety you do so well. I wonder if the medium is capable of expressing what you want to say. If it's powerful enough. There seems to be a violence here that you're not expressing properly." He stops talking and stoops down to peer at my painting—one of the rainy, bluish ones. "But this is in so many ways extraordinary, Christine. You astonish me."

Emile has changed his tune. For the first couple of weeks he gave me good constructive advice during critiques. "Attack the canvas!" he said. "Don't skimp on the colors. Give up some of your control, let the paper and the paint do some of the work and then go with it!" Now he touches my arm, puts his hand on my shoulder as he leans over the table where I work, looks at my breasts when he talks to me, tells me my work is exquisite. The other students notice. A girl named Diane tells me he's famous for screwing his students. "Not that he's not attractive," Diane says. "But."

I hate everything I do in the course, but he gives me an A. The day it's over, he asks me if I will do him the honor of dining with him. He dazzles me. He is tall, lean, distinguished. He has a small, foreign-looking beard, a thin moustache. He smokes Gauloises and calls me *chérie*. Three months later, we are married. Not long after that, he begins again to find fault with my painting, and he looks at the breasts of other women.

～

Dear *Maman*,

I look forward so much to coming to New Haven. I love Paris, and I have the intent to settle here when I finish school, but I think I need some sort of change, and I miss you and *Grand'-mère* Silvie very much. Papa is preoccupied with Nicole, as you might think, with the wedding just several months down the road. I actually like her quite a bit, though she does keep him busy. I think he neglects his new book, which he has a contract for. Fortunately, I have so much to do I'm not at home so much. I'm playing, believe this or not, American baseball, we have formed a team at the *lycée,* just for fun. That plus orchestra practice plus just seeing friends. Also I am interested in the *Jeunesse Socialiste,* and our meetings are often in the evening. Still, I have never liked coming home to an empty place. Two friends of mine are also applying to Yale, we have high hope, me especially because of you living so close by . . .

～

He had just closed a big deal, and he was in a good mood. We sat in the Metro, drinking beer and eating nachos. Afterward, he said, we could go someplace and dance, or listen to some jazz. I had no desire to do that: I felt at home in the Metro, with its noisy bar and our quiet booth in the back—the same one we sat in before. The tabletop was heavily carved with initials, like a school desk. VINCE '76, it said. TOM + BARBARA. JAGUAR. BABY. H.K. + G.G. The light from the Tiffany lamp was dim and pinkish. Orin wore a brown suit of soft, subtle tweed, an off-white shirt with the collar loosened, a brown and red regimental tie. I thought of James in his apron, when I kissed him good-bye before I left for the train. He was growing out one skinny hank of hair at the back of his head—Raymond's idea. "One last fling before you're middle-aged, man," Raymond said. It was almost long enough to braid. "Will I look like an asshole, Chris?" he'd asked me that morning. "Tell me honestly."

Under the table, Orin's knee touched mine. "Excuse me," he said, and moved it away. As we sat in the Metro and talked, I became fascinated with his suit, the subtle heathery tweed of his sleeve, his lapel, the faint blue interwoven with the browns, the Impressionist look of the minute dots of color artfully blended. It occurred to me that, if someone had told me that Pierce was alive and well and living in New York, this was not the way I would have pictured him: not in this exquisite suit, this perfectly coordinated tie. Not going to meetings of the Landmark Preservation Society. Not talking about interest rates and the Fed. Maybe in a loft, in SoHo or NoHo, living with artists. Maybe in a dark club somewhere, being outrageous. Maybe on a corner, playing a guitar, with a cigar box for money at his feet. Maybe dealing drugs. Maybe panhandling at Grand Central. And then I saw how unfair I was being to him, and I experienced a fresh pang of sorrow for his loss—the loss of Pierce and all his possibilities, the loss of any chance he might have had to change, to become his true self, to pass through that awkward, terrible time that had all of us in its grip and come out like—like Orin, maybe, after all. Like this man who was so at home in his beautiful clothes.

We talked about this and that—anything. I liked being with him when I could forget what had brought us together—something that happened only for brief moments. It was hard to concentrate because

I had to keep studying him. He no longer looked like Pierce to me, and yet he reminded me of Pierce in some elusive, indefinable way that had nothing to do with his actual features, and I kept trying to figure out what it was. I would be sure (*he is not Pierce*), most of the time I was sure (*this is Orin, someone entirely different*), and then it would happen: he would laugh at something I said, and pour beer into his glass, lowering his head, and there it was: the sly amusement, the lifted eyebrow: the phantom Pierce-ness that took over his face at unexpected moments. I knew it was illusion, coincidence, a temporary trick of the light and the angle and his bone structure, but it was very powerful, as powerful as anything in Proust to evoke the past. He lowered his head, lifted his eyebrow, and I was eighteen, I was twenty-three, a wind-up penguin waddled in circles, I sat in a bar called Tynan's, I walked down a cold Ohio street—and it was Pierce sitting there across from me.

The indecision I felt was sickening, a feeling I compared to one of those brutal rides I used to force myself to go on at the Jamesville Fair when I was a kid: the swoops up, and back down, the spins, the desperate desire to get back on land, to be still.

Or the time, in college, when my period was three weeks late and I didn't know what to do. I went around for a few days in a fog of misery while I sensed something growing in me, cells implacably dividing, and dividing again. I cut classes and walked the streets of Oberlin, Ohio, in the bitter February wind that used to sweep down all the way from Lake Erie, ten miles north. I kept imagining marrying Charlie (knowing for the first time how sincerely I didn't want to do that), or having to get myself to Puerto Rico or somewhere for an abortion, or dropping out of school at twenty to become somebody's mother. I felt as if the world had shut me out—there was no place for me in it: none of my choices contained the slightest degree of hope. I began to think of myself as a doomed person. The need to know became imperative; there would be comfort in certainty. I took a bus to Elyria for a pregnancy test. By the time the results were available, I'd gotten my period. What I retained from the experience was the sense of groping in the dark, of being sure of nothing, of feeling that the bottom of the universe had been pulled out from under my feet.

He said, eventually, "I take it you no longer want to ask me questions."

The amused curl to his mouth: that was Pierce. I looked down at the scarred table top, knowing that when I raised my head again the illusion would be gone. I felt dizzy. JAGUAR. BABY. VINCE '76. All around me, the Metro was filled with people having normal conversations.

"You could, you know," he said. "There are plenty of questions you could ask."

Who are you?

What am I doing?

How did I get to this point?

Why am I sitting in this bar with a man who wears these clothes?

"Go ahead. Ask me anything, Christine. Really."

"No," I said—immediately, without having to think. There are, after all, worse things in the world than indecision. "I have no questions."

"I can get hold of my college yearbook. Columbia, Class of 1964. I could get a copy of my birth certificate. I could get the IBM Corporation in St. Louis to certify that I was working for them when I was supposed to be living in New Haven going to drama school or whatever. I could get Mr. Thompson from the music department at St. Paul's to swear to you that I can't carry a tune."

"No," I said. "I have no questions."

"You're convinced? Promise?"

"Yes. Promise."

Under the table, our legs touched again, he parted my legs with his knee, rubbed his wooly, tweedy knee against the inside of my thigh. This should be enough, I told myself: this warmth, this man's attention, his easy company, the tiny thrill of meeting him in secret. It would be good for my painting, this new dimension to my life. It might even be good for James and me, maybe we were getting too stale and domestic.

He said, "So it's just the two of us, Christine. Just you and me."

I thought: Remember that time in New York, at your cousin's place in the Village, when we almost ended up in bed together?

I looked at the light in his eyes and nodded.

~

A couple of months after Pierce quits the Yale School of Drama (or is asked to leave, he never makes it really clear) he takes a job in a bank. They send him to Springfield for a two-week training program, and when he comes back he's a teller, with a wood-grain nameplate that says MR. PIERCE. He demonstrates to me how he can count off a hundred bills, fast and accurately, without licking his thumb. When he gets fired from that job, he collects unemployment.

Charlie is still in Philadelphia then, living in an apartment with people he doesn't much like and working in a drugstore. I'm living in Mount Joy, not far from there. My old friend Bridget and I have jobs as waitresses in her grandmother's Pennsylvania Dutch–style restaurant. I'm no longer involved with Charlie—he has a girlfriend named Leah, I'm going out with the bartender at the Dutch Farms Inn—but we're thinking of going to graduate school together, maybe to Cornell, maybe to Michigan. We both have the idea that we're getting nowhere, pissing away our lives, living like irresponsible children while the world passes us by.

Every once in a while, I get a ride to Philly, and Charlie and I take the train to New Haven for a weekend. Pierce meets us at the station in his VW, and we go to his place on Orange Street and smoke dope and drink beer and listen to music and laugh at Pierce's wicked imitations of the people at the drama school and then at the bank and then in the unemployment line. He has given up the guitar, but he and Charlie still sing Everly Brothers songs. We go down to Tynan's and meet Pierce's friends. We roam the streets of New Haven, or buy popcorn and sit on a bench on the Green feeding the pigeons. Sometimes we go to a movie. Once, in the summer, we drive out to Hammonasset Beach, not far from Pierce's parents' place, though Pierce hates his home town, refuses to go swimming, and, while Charlie and I fool around in the waves, he walks down to the far end of the beach where he sits on the rocks, smoking, with his feet in the water.

But mostly we just sit around Pierce's apartment and get drunk, and when we can't stay awake any longer we all fall asleep on Pierce's living room floor.

Then, going home hung over on the train to Pennsylvania, Charlie and I have long, serious conversations about how we need to get control of things, and about how Pierce is screwing up. "His trouble is, he's too good at too many things," Charlie says once. "That must be confusing." This is a typical Charlie remark.

When his unemployment runs out, Pierce gets a new job, in the hi-fi department at Sears. He talks himself into some kind of managerial position, and the pay is good. He buys us presents: the Van Gogh letters for me, a fancy pipe for Charlie. He gives his current girlfriend gold hoop earrings. Then he shows us what he has bought for himself: a .38 Smith & Wesson Special.

~

"You two must have been related," I said to Orin. "The resemblance really is uncanny, especially combined with the coincidence of the names."

"Separated at birth," he said, with his Pierce grin. "The question is, which one of us was stolen away by the gypsies?"

When I showed him the snapshots, he said, "This is Pierce? This guy?" He shook his head slowly form side to side, frowning. "I just can't see it, Christine. I don't know what to say. This guy looks nothing like me."

When he raised his eyes to my face, he looked exactly like Pierce.

~

Plover Island is a mile across, the largest and farthest from shore of a group of eight or ten stony outcroppings off the Maine coast near Camden. Several of them are uninhabitable—too tiny, too rocky, their very existence too precarious—but on some islands there are buildings, and on at least two there are elaborate modern houses, with generators and plumbing and expensive lawn furniture brought over from the mainland.

Plover Island has several cottages, widely spaced, and a rough wooden dock. My father's brother, Uncle Bill, built a primitive cabin there when he was a young man. He was a research chemist who lived outside Boston, and he spent summers on the island until he died. He and my father weren't very friendly. I think my father had been there only twice before he inherited the place. Bill was a lifelong bachelor. He didn't particularly like people, and he detested children. (Robbie and I were never invited to Maine.) But he died just after I graduated from college, and since he had no one else, he left the Plover Island place to us.

It's exciting to own a piece of an island, however rocky and insignificant, but it's hard for my parents to get away. In warm weather, the motel business is booming on Route 92. The four of us drive up there together only once—a weekend early in that first summer. My mother hates roughing it, the neglected cabin appalls her, and after one night in sleeping bags she and I get on the morning ferry. Robbie teases us, but Dad is angry. Mom and I check into a motel in Camden that has a whirlpool bath and beds with Magic Fingers. We go out for a lobster dinner, and my mother drinks a lot of wine. Her exhilaration frightens me a little—her delight in defying my father. The next day, while we wait for the ferry to bring them back, she and I go shopping. She buys a wickerwork purse decorated with shells, and a white cotton jersey with fishnet sleeves. She wants to buy me a t-shirt with a picture of a lobster on it but I decline, so she buys it for Robbie. We sit on a bench near the town dock waiting for them and eating pastel-colored salt water taffy. On the long, tense ride home I get carsick and throw everything up.

My parents keep talking about enlarging the cabin and making improvements, but for the moment my mother is glad to stay home, and at that time in my life I have better things to do than take vacations with my family.

But Robbie and my father fall in love with the place. They have spent most of Robbie's teenage years fighting—the usual arguments over music, curfew, car. It wasn't terrible, but it was bad enough; at its worst, Robbie moved out and lived with his friend Mark's family for a month. My father has never been the world's most amiable man, even on a good day. He has a few things in common with his brother Bill. But on the island a spell is cast over them both. They become what they have never been before: buddies. They fish, sit in the sun drinking beer, listen to staticy baseball on Robbie's portable radio, play endless games of frisbee and two-handed poker.

"You may not believe this, but Dad is actually not a bad guy," is the way Robbie puts it to me. But for a brief, strange, wonderful period, the trips to Maine change my father's life.

"I've got my boy back," he says to my mother after their first trip together. He has dropped Robbie off at Dartmouth and come home filthy, sunburned, sand in his hair, his clothes stinking of fish. "I was beginning to think I'd lost the kid for good," he says. "But it's like old times. It's better than old times, because we really talked to each other. We really *listened* to each other, that was the amazing thing."

My mother tells me about this conversation the day after Robbie's funeral—about Dad's fishy clothes, and how for days after he got home she would catch him grinning at nothing. "I don't know if I ever saw your father so happy before," she says. "I didn't care if I ever set foot on that island again, but I have to admit I was a little jealous."

But things get cool again between Dad and Robbie. Their arguments are predictable and inevitable, given the times, given their personalities, and no number of fishing trips can change things. They disagree about the war in Vietnam, about Nixon, about Robbie's ponytail, about the girl he brings briefly home on semester break that year. My mother is worried about Robbie; he is flunking chemistry, flunking German; he looks thin and unkempt; he is silent and withdrawn. When classes let out, he heads straight for Maine. He says he's spending the summer in the cabin, alone. He needs to think, to get his head straight. My father hates that expression, he hates all Robbie's trendy slang, and he makes fun of it mercilessly. "He'd get his head a lot straighter if he'd cut off some of that hair." My father is also angry that Robbie won't be working—both of us have been encouraged to work since the days of baby-sitting and paper routes—but Robbie has a job during the school year in the dining hall at Dartmouth and makes plenty of money, so there's not a lot Dad can say. Robbie says he's going to write some poetry. Take some photographs. Get in touch with nature. Figure things out.

My mother worries all summer—that summer I'm home working in the motel and mourning Pierce. There isn't so much as a postcard from Robbie. One of my mother's fears is that he has some girl with him and he'll get her pregnant, but her greatest fear, the one that keeps her awake at night, is that he'll flunk out of school and be drafted. My father says, "*That* would put his head straight for him all right." We watch the Democratic Convention on television, the riots, the police bashing long-haired boys like Robbie over the head, and my mother says, "I suppose I should be thankful he's safe up in

Maine."

His body isn't discovered until late in August. One of the islanders calls the Maine State Police, they notify the Jamesville police, and we get the news from Ralph Jarrett, whose wife taught both Robbie and me in third grade, and whose daughters worked at our motel as maids all through high school. Ralph rings the bell late one hot afternoon, refuses the lemonade my mother offers, and says, "I sure wish I didn't have to be the one to tell you people this." His voice breaks. I'm standing in the middle of the kitchen. I push past Ralph and out the door, and head down to the pond where I watch the water-striders skim over its silver surface.

After the funeral, my mother goes through a period where she needs to talk about Robbie all the time, mostly reminiscences of his babyhood, his boyhood. I'm the one who has to listen to her, to cry with her at the kitchen table, passing the tissue box back and forth; it's one reason I leave home again and go back to live in New Haven. My father quits talking completely unless it's absolutely necessary, and he never speaks my brother's name again until that New Year's Eve when he calls James Robbie by mistake.

~

"If this were a movie, I would be the victim of a conspiracy. You and Alison Kaye would be in it together. Alison and her Filo-Fax would have been intentional—I was meant to see it, she sat down next to me deliberately. And the Mr. Pierce thing at the Frick was staged. And you knew me so well, you knew I'd pursue it."

"I'm Pierce, and I staged my own death, and I've been biding my time all these years, cooking up this deal with Alison—and who else? The Mafia? The CIA? The PLO?"

"Sure. Why not? This is a movie."

"And what's the point of it all?" he asked. The Pierce smile on his face. "What's behind this crazy scheme?"

We were in the Metro. I was wearing new clothes: a silk paisley skirt and a long-sleeved blouse with what the saleswoman called Cossack sleeves. I had spent a day prowling Macy's and the Hello Boutique and the new, cute little shops on Chapel Street, and I had come away with a dress, a couple of skirts, blouses, a tailored jacket, sheer pale stockings, and leather: honey-colored shoes with little heels, and a soft brown bag like a mailman's. I hadn't worn leather in years. James admired the clothes, and his only comment about my buying leather again was, "So who can be perfect in an imperfect world?"

I felt good dressed up, looking normal. I felt pretty. I smiled back at Orin and said, "You're probably involved in a plot to defraud me out of my fortune."

"You don't have a fortune."

"If this were a movie, I would."

He did something he had never done: leaned across the table and kissed me.

I said, "I wish this were that movie, Pierce. I really do. I'd hand it over to you without a struggle."

He said, "Christine."

I said, "I'm sorry."

~

I begin by plaiting what Mrs. Spooler calls a cookie server out of folded strips of newspaper, but she sees I have a knack for it and lets me go on to a simple splint basket of flat reed. Then I make a cheese basket and a series of potato baskets. I learn fancy splintwork, the Deerfield border, advanced coiling (lazy squaw, Peruvian coil) based on Native American techniques. I make ribbed melon baskets, which are tricky, and a large clothes hamper. My hands become raw from working with wet reed. Mrs. Spooler says no one in her experience with craft therapy has ever caught on so fast, or made so many baskets in such a short time.

The time doesn't seem short to me. I'm in the hospital for three months, and in that time I see Denis only once. Emile is divorcing me. He is taking Denis with him to France. *Lucy's Pup,* not yet published, has already been sold to publishers in England, France, West Germany, Sweden, Japan. Emile comes to see me, tells me he is taking Denis, tells me exactly why.

"Are you going to contest it?" he asks me.

I only look at him. "What do you think?" I know Denis is better off with him, though I can't believe Emile loves our son more than I do, or as much. I don't know whether to believe it or not when he tells me Denis doesn't ask for me.

That's all I say: "What do you think?"—wearily, from my chair by the window that looks out on the parking lot, the brown roofs of New Haven, the smoky blue sky over Long Island Sound. I cried all the time when we got back from Plover Island—that's partly why I'm here—and I still cry constantly, but I stop when Emile visits me. The sound of his voice, the things he accuses me of—all of this numbs me, gives me a kind of peace. He leaves, and his footsteps going away down the hall say to me that I have lost my son. I begin crying again.

Basket-weaving is such a cliché, such a joke, but I can't deny that it's both restful and involving. It soothes me better than any medication. Sometimes I think I shouldn't let myself be soothed, I should get help. Mrs. Spooler, Dr. Dalziel, Silvie—someone should know what Emile is doing. But there seems no point. I know that I don't deserve to have Denis. It's true that I'm unstable, I'm a bad mother, I'm good for nothing but sitting in a chair looking out the window, or making baskets. I have no idea what I'll do when I leave the hospital, or where I'll go. I have few friends, my parents aren't nearby, my husband has left me, my son is gone.

I think constantly of Denis. I also think of Pierce, and of the visitation from Robbie. For years I wondered, and now my mind has been set at rest. Pierce is blameless: he remains my perfect, my own Pierce. My son is gone, but I have drunk tea with my brother, and Pierce has been returned to me.

I weave the wet, flat reed into shapes that please me. I learn twining and make raffia baskets with covers that fit precisely. I make a series of Shaker baskets in graduated sizes. I stop the constant weeping that has accompanied everything I do. I can eat the wretched hospital food. I sleep better. When I get a copy of *Lucy's Pup* in the mail (with a printed card inside that says "Compliments of the Author"), all that's left to me is a distant, desperate wish that I had a child on my lap to read it to.

~

Hugh invited James and me out to his place for dinner one night. He said that he and Helga wanted our advice: they were thinking of moving in together, and they were scared stiff.

"You're our ideal couple," Helga said to me on the phone. "Tell us how you do it."

Helga was blonde and glamorous and a fund-raiser for one of the New Haven theaters; Hugh was a scruffy carpenter with a passion for stray cats. They seemed an unlikely couple—though perhaps no less odd than a watercolorist and an ex-accountant turned pizzateur.

"She'll have a hell of a commute," James said as we drove up to Hugh's place. He had ten hilly acres in an area north and west of New Haven, miles from the nearest highway. "That's the only drawback that I can see."

It was a Sunday night. When my train had gotten in the night before, I went straight to Jimmy Luigi's. My trips to New York were beginning to makes James uneasy: he was quiet and wary with me, and curious, though he wouldn't question me directly. While he ladled out sauce and sprinkled cheese, I told him in detail about George's reaction to my new group of slides. The truth was that I had talked briefly to George (who was interested but distant) from the phone booth at the Metro. With James, I made George into a joke. I exaggerated, I went too far. I could feel this happening, but I was unable to stop it. James looked at me oddly—I kept getting the feeling he was watching for me to slip up—though the only questions he asked me were practical ones about the possibilities for a show at the Aurora.

In the Metro, a tall, skinny black man who looked like Raymond walked toward our booth, and I put the menu in front of my face. "It's a big town," Orin said, taking it away. "Do you know what your chances are of being seen with me?"

It wasn't Raymond, anyway. Then, walking through Central Park, I thought I saw Silvie.

"Relax," Orin kept saying. "I'm your cousin, I'm an old college chum you ran into at the Modern, I'm the husband of some friend of yours and we're on our way to pick her up. What's the matter? Don't you have any instinct for this sort of thing?"

I thought of my frantic fabrications about George Drescher. "I'm not much of a liar."

He squeezed my arm. "Stick with me, baby."

James exited off Route 8 and drove toward the minor highway that led to the back road that would take us to the lightless road that petered out to dirt just before Hugh's place. "What should we advise?" James asked me. "Do it or not?"

"We're their ideal couple," I said. "If we say do it, they probably will. It's a heavy responsibility."

"So what do you think?" He looked sideways at me, quickly, then back to the dark road.

I turned toward him on the seat and pulled his little pigtail. "Sure," I said. I wanted so much to be natural and affectionate with him. "Why not? We're doing all right, aren't we?"

He reached over and patted me on the knee through my jeans. I could see him grin. His relief filled the car. "I think so," he said. And then he took a breath and added, "Maybe we should surprise Hugh and Helga. Maybe we should announce that we're actually going to get married."

"Is this a proposal?" My voice was fond and playful, and I listened to it with contempt. I looked out the car window at the black night. In the darkness, everything was menacing, it was impossible to see how beautiful it was out there: classic New England, with stone fences and red barns and trees just coming into leaf. I had spent a whole sleepless night after my return from New York trying to think of a way to tell James we should split up; now the idea filled me with terror.

"It's more of an attempt to open a discussion," he said. "What do you think, love?"

Love. I thought; I don't deserve to marry James. I sniffed back tears. I was afraid that if I cried and he comforted me, I would tell him everything. Tell him what? I never think about you any more, I never think about anything but this man, I sit in bars with him, we kiss, he might be Pierce, he isn't Pierce, he reminds me of Pierce, he brings Pierce back to me. He brings back my youth, James: maybe it's that simple.

I said, "I've been thinking about Emile a lot, lately, maybe because of the possibility of Denis coming to Yale. That whole thing—I know it was years ago, James, but—it just made me feel so wary of marriage. I can't help it, I associate marriage with Emile. With various kinds of betrayal, I guess. I think I just need more time."

The more I talked, the more I felt like slime, like garbage, like something subhuman: I felt like the time Bridget made me flush her ailing fish down the toilet—a red Siamese fighting fish who had fought himself into a nasty, incurable case of the ick. I could remember how he had leapt in disbelief, in protest, in pain at the coldness of the water. "I know it was the humane thing to do," Bridget had said. "But better you than me. You've got the stomach for things like that."

James was silent for a moment. He said, "You've been divorced twelve years."

"Eleven. Twelve next October."

"How long do you think it'll take you to get over it?"

"Oh, James—"

"I'm sorry," he said. He touched my knee again. "I'm sorry, Chris. Believe me, I'm not underestimating what that bastard put you through. All that stuff with Denis. Taking advantage of your mental state. I can see where it would take a while to get over that. I just think we belong together. Lately I've had this feeling that I'm losing you, you're so wrapped up in your painting. And I've been thinking about this a lot. Let me just say that whenever you're ready, I'd like to do it. Get married."

I couldn't stop myself from crying, and he pulled over and took me in his arms. I remembered the day we met, how lonely we both were, how he took so seriously the idea that a couple of cats were what I needed. I cried as if some physical problem had just been fixed that had kept me from weeping all my life.

"I'm sorry if I've neglected you," I said finally.

"It's nothing," he insisted. He took a tissue from his pocket and wiped my eyes with it. "It's just all these trips to New York, and you seem to use your painting to get away from me. I know that's silly, I know I'm imagining things. I must be having a belated mid-life crisis."

I blew my nose and sat up straight. I felt that if I let myself I could sit there and cry for a week. I could think of nothing to say except the truth, and I had a moment of panic. Then I said, "I think it's partly that Denis is coming here. It's on my mind a lot. Let me get used to motherhood before I think about marriage."

"Like the Virgin Mary had to do."

I smiled over at him. "You must admit it's going to be a huge change for all of us."

He handed me another tissue: he was the kind of man who offered cats in a crisis, who always had clean tissues in his pocket. "And you don't like change," he said. "How well I know."

Now he was going to tease me: we had argued for weeks the previous fall about moving Jimmy Luigi's farther up Chapel Street to a historic building that was being restored. We'd lose half our clientele, I told him: kids, shoppers from the Mall, people changing buses or coming from events on the Green. His position was that we'd get more Yalies, more faculty, plus the museum crowd and the yuppies. I said that the yuppies and the Yalies would move down because the pizza was so great, but our regular customers would never move up. James said that might sound like a great sociological insight, but it was just a coverup for the fact that I was a hopeless curmudgeon, set in my ways worse than his Aunt Gert had ever been.

"Of course you were right about the move," he said. "I walk by the restaurants in the new building all the time, and I never see anybody in there." He put the car in gear and we proceeded down the road toward Hugh's place. "Why are you always right? And you're right about this, too. We can wait. We're fine the way we are. One upheaval at a time. Do you think the kid will report everything back to that Frenchie swine? Tell him I need to lose thirty pounds and I have a pigtail and smell of oregano and I'm always nagging you to marry me?"

I laughed and took his hand, and we held hands as he drove. I thought, fiercely: I won't see Orin any more, I don't need to see Orin, the next time he calls I'll tell him it can't go on. I knew perfectly well that this wasn't true, but for the moment it was better to believe it was.

We all got very merry over dinner, and I advised Hugh and Helga to go ahead, live together, take us as their ideal couple if they wanted to because that's exactly what we were, we were even thinking of getting married as soon as things calmed down a little bit. James beamed at me, his dark eyes soft with contentment. I drank enough wine so that the last leap of that fish no longer haunted me, I no longer even thought about it. It was James who said it: Who can be perfect in an imperfect world?

~

It's early summer when Emile and I take Denis to Plover Island. My parents have never gotten rid of the cabin: in order to sell it, they would have had to talk about it, and they never do—at least, my father never does. Every year, my mother writes a check for the taxes on the place. I told her once that I was glad they still owned it, that it seemed to me a sort of memorial to Robbie—I didn't like the idea of selling it to some jolly family who would spruce it up and have good times there. My mother just looked at me.

No one but seagulls, as far as I know, has been there in the nearly eight years since Robbie shot himself.

"It's ridiculous," Emile has been saying almost since we were married. "There's this incredibly beautiful island, your family actually owns a piece of it, and nobody ever goes there."

He won't let it be. He's always trying to convince me of things, most of them outrageous. We should move to France, we should buy the red MG convertible he saw at an auto show, we should start looking now for a horse farm in Virginia to possibly retire to someday.

This is not outrageous, Emile says. It makes sense. Why should we pay so much for vacations? We shell out money to go to Vermont for a week every summer, or to the Cape, and here's Plover Island for free. He appreciates what we've all been through, he can even understand why my parents don't want to set foot in the place—but why couldn't we just go up for a weekend? Yes, the memories might be disturbing, it would be a sad pilgrimage, he can see that. But eight years have gone by, and he'll be with me, and little Denis would love it so much.

"We'll exorcise all the ghosts, Christine," he says to me. "It will do you good to face this."

He says these things to me over and over, and finally we drive up the day after Denis's day-care center closes for the summer. A man named Tom, from the marina in Camden, takes us to the island in his outboard. Emile talks about getting a boat, he asks Tom's advice, he tries to sound knowledgeable. There is a ferry, Tom tells us, and if we intend to become regulars we can arrange for it to make stops until we get ourselves a boat. I remember the ferry from the time my mother and I retreated to the motel; it must have run more regularly then. I tell Tom the story, and he laughs, slapping his thigh with his huge red hand. (Denis watches him, slaps his own skinny little thigh.) Tom tells us about the other people who live on the island—mostly old-timers who have been coming there for years. He says nothing about our place, the tragedy, though he must be aware of it.

"First time up here for me and the boy," Emile says. "And my wife's only been here once, years ago."

"Twice, actually."

"Twice?" He gives me a look. I stare down into the ridged green water. I wonder if, later, or tomorrow, he'll ask me to explain—if he cares enough to do that. I wonder what I would say.

Denis puts out his hand and laughs when the icy spray soaks his whole arm, his sleeve.

The island seems new to me: I'm used to the tamer coast of Connecticut, the Sound. I've forgotten what real ocean is like, the rocky wildness of it. The day is overcast, rain threatening, and the cold, choppy sea that exhilarates Denis frightens me. Even the cabin seems like a wild place, something made by nature—a pile of driftwood thrown up by the waves. Tom says, "I'll see you folks tomorrow, I should be getting here around three," and we wave at him from the dock, Emile holding Denis up so he can watch the boat become a speck in the distance.

"I like Tom," Denis says.

"Someday we'll have a boat just like his," Emile tells him. "Maybe bigger." I imagine the boat replacing the MG and the apartment in Paris.

He agrees to approach the cabin first. Denis and I wait out on the rocks, watching the sea birds gather on the beach below us. Denis asks me what they are. I tell him I don't know. Plovers, maybe. In his solemn, scholarly way, he says, "I want to find out." My son has immediately adopted the place, and I try to imagine coming here summer after summer—becoming *regulars*. The desolation seems immutable: can we really keep it at bay with lamps and lawn chairs? I turn my back to the cabin, and to the frightening immensity beyond it, and I keep my eyes on the mainland where I can see a motel sign, the spire of a church, the marina with its litter of boats.

Emile shouts from the cabin, beckons us with his arm. "It's okay," he says when we reach him—meaning that there is nothing I need to fear, no traces of Robbie. We go in: dust and mildew and mouse droppings. The spider webs that drape the windows and hang from the ceilings are delicately beautiful in the light. The windows have stayed intact, and there is surprisingly little damage. Someone has cleaned up—maybe the police, or maybe time has kindly erased whatever Robbie left behind: food, bloodstains, books, the stink of a rotting corpse.

In the doorway, Emile looks questioningly into my eyes.

"I'm all right," I tell him.

"You sound surprised."

"I dreaded this. I thought it would be horrible. But it's fine, I have almost no memory of this place. It's good to be here." I have to force myself to say that. It's not entirely true. But inside is, strangely, better than outside.

"I shouldn't have made you come." It's his way, to get what he wants and then apologize and be extra nice. "Forgive me," he says. "I really wanted to see it. And it's what I expected, it's wonderful. Look at Denis, he loves it already." He hugs me. "And it's just for this one night. Just check it out."

We are planning to sleep on the island, then continue by car across the state of Maine and into Quebec where Denis can hear French spoken.

"You're sure it's okay?"

"I'm sure."

We have brought a bag of cleaning supplies, and we clean. Denis would prefer to be outside in the wind, picking up thumbnail shells on the beach or exploring the jagged shelf of rock that extends from the cabin door down to the dock. But we keep him with us, and he amuses himself knocking down cobwebs with the toy broom we brought for him. He has no fear of anything—spiders, rocks, the ocean rolling up to the shore, the overcast sky. We have to watch him every minute.

The cabin is small, just two rooms divided by a flimsy partition.

There is no plumbing and no outhouse, but we find some dishes and glasses neatly put away in a mouseproof metal box, and a chamberpot in a corner of the far room. (Denis is enchanted with the idea of a chamberpot, and immediately piddles, then toddles outside to empty it under a prickly bush we don't know the name of.) There are two camp chairs, an ancient wicker armchair, a wooden stool, a stand with a drawer in it, a rickety table with mouse-gnawed legs, and a crude bookcase probably made by Uncle Bill. There are no books in it. In the drawer of the stand, Denis finds a rabbit's foot: the fur has moldered away except for one white tuft, and what's left are the long bones of the foot, as crisp and dainty as the hand of an elegant doll.

When darkness approaches, the wind dies down and a belated red sun comes out. The air warms up. We have a picnic on the beach: bread, cheese, salami. Emile and I have wine. From here, none of the cottages are visible. The beach is clean and windswept, but it seems creepy to me, not because of Robbie but because of the isolation: we have seen no other people, no boats. The sky presses down. The sun makes a path like fire across the water. The scene suggests a movie to me: something coming up out of the water, some evil presence.

I can almost, almost understand why Robbie chose this particular place to do what he did.

Denis runs until he's exhausted, and then he asks questions: How did the mice get here? Can we build a lookout in that big tree? How much did Tom's boat cost? Why do we have to put in a toilet? What are the birds doing now? What's this? What's that?

We watch the sun begin to set behind the church steeple and the motels. Denis can hardly stay awake long enough to use the chamber pot again. Long before dark, we put him to sleep in his Big Bird sleeping bag. He passes out instantly, and Emile and I make love in the outer room. For a while, we're fond of each other (this is a feeling that comes and goes), and we fall asleep in each other's arms.

I dream of water, of going under again and again, of green darkness and no air, of water invading my lungs and eyes and veins, and I wake up screaming.

～

Dear *Maman,*

By now you must be knowing the Yale news. This is certainly super! Although it is hard to believe that I will be really living in America, only a few five or six months away from now. It will be good to be in your city, which Papa has told me is not such a great city, but I have a feeling I will like it. How much crime and danger is there? Papa says these are excessive. However, these are not the kinds of things I consider worries. The Yale photos make it look very beautiful. Do you have further Yale photos besides the ones they send? I like very much to see more, I like to look at my new home. *Maman,* I look forward to seeing you so much, and I am told the Yale band is a very good one, a very funny place to be in . . .

~

I told James I was sick of coming home on the late train. I told him I might even find a way to stay overnight sometimes. I told him that I needed to be more adventurous. I told him that if I were ever going to make it as a painter I needed to be more in touch with what other painters were doing. I told him my visits to the museums and galleries gave me more energy to paint. I told him I'd been stuck out in the boonies too long.

He asked me, "Are you having an affair with that fucking Drescher?"

~

Pierce picks up a sturdy old picnic basket at a junk shop in Manlius, and we take it with us up to Plover Island. Charlie is supposed to go too, but his grandfather has died and he has to be home with his family, so it's just Pierce and Robbie and me in Pierce's VW.

Charlie and Pierce are rooming together in New Haven, thinking about joining the Peace Corps or hitchhiking through Europe. Pierce is between jobs, and he's been staying with us in Jamesville that summer for a couple of weeks, working at the motel and refusing to take any salary—a fact that almost succeeds in impressing my father, who is not an easy man to impress.

When we pull out of the driveway, Dad says, "Have fun, kids. I wish I was going with you," and he punches Robbie on the arm. "We'll have to get up there again before the end of the summer, you and me."

Robbie says, "Sure, Dad. Why not?"

In the picnic basket Pierce has packed a fifth of vodka, a fifth of tequila, a small plastic bag of marijuana, and a hash pipe.

Pierce drinks a lot of vodka in the car. We play Botticelli, and when Pierce gets drunk enough he sings "Bull Cow Blues" and "You Can't Tell the Difference After Dark" and "Please Warm My Weiner." He buys me the wind-up penguin in a souvenir shop in Ogunquit when we stop for food. We sit in a diner where the penguin keeps walking off the tabletop and Robbie and I try to force Pierce to drink black coffee. Pierce pulls over outside Portland and tells me I'd better drive. In the back seat, Robbie sits slumped with his eyes half-closed, smoking my cigarettes and trying not to show how relieved he is.

We've missed the last ferry, and we have to pay a preppy couple at the marina ten dollars to let us leave the car there and then take us out to the island. They bitch all the way about what a favor they're doing us, and about how some kids trashed somebody's summer place on one of the other islands. Robbie tries to make conversation with them. Pierce sits in silence, smoking, looking bored and gloomy.

The island is a dark, angular shape against a dark sky. When we arrive, there is very little light left. All three of us stumble getting out of the boat, and end up soaked to the knees. The mosquitoes are fierce, and we're too loaded down with bags and duffels to swat at them.

But we cheer up when we get to the cabin. It's in good shape. Since our disastrous family trip, my father and Robbie have been there several times, and they have left lanterns, a charcoal grill and a bag of briquettes, a couple of cheap aluminum lawn chairs, some cushions, an L.L. Bean catalog, and a book called *A Guide to the Atlantic Seacoast*. There is a jug of bottled water, enough beef jerky for an army, and a roll of toilet paper for each chamber pot.

Pierce looks around with approval and says, "What a dump! What movie is that from?"—which is roughly the first line from *Who's Afraid of Virginia Woolf?* in which he once almost got the part of George.

Robbie is glad to be out of Pierce's car, and he laughs at all his jokes. We have brought steaks, which we cook on the grill by the light of two kerosene lanterns. It takes forever, and by the time they're ready we are almost too tired to eat. We go inside, and while Robbie goes back out for his duffel, Pierce suddenly, out of the blue, kisses me. We would share a sleeping bag if Robbie wasn't there; that, at least, is what we say, standing there half asleep with our arms around each other. "We're doomed never to make it," Pierce says.

"We haven't really tried all that hard," I point out.

"Maybe we think about it too much," Pierce says.

This is one of those remarks I will mull over for a long time: I will pull it apart and analyze it endlessly before I figure out that it really doesn't mean much.

I put my head on his shoulder. He smells like kerosene and charcoal smoke.

The next day I walk around the island sketching while Pierce and Robbie mess around: they're like little boys, they build a fort out of driftwood, they try to identify different kinds of seaweed with the guidebook, they catch crabs and then don't know what to do with them. I meet another artist on my walk, a woman in a smock with an easel set up on a rocky point. She and I smile shyly but don't speak. I meet a couple of red-faced old men who tell me they're brothers, both retired, both widowed, they spend every summer on the island. They look like fishermen, but one was a pharmacist and the other an insurance executive. The pharmacist gives me three plums.

For lunch we have plums and beef jerky and cold canned stew and tequila. We sit in the hot sun on the rocky, sandy beach. Robbie dozes off, and I begin doing drawings of the patterns the seaweed makes drying on the sand. Pierce gets bored and goes inside for the picnic basket. He takes out the pipe, but neither of us is in the mood, and then he takes out a paper bag, and inside it is the .38, wrapped in a red bandanna.

I feel no fear, we've been friends so long, but the gun makes me uneasy. He has changed since college. His life is no longer going well. For years, he got what he wanted, or nearly: Oberlin instead of Harvard, B's instead of A's—Horatio instead of Hamlet, perhaps, but still a great part. Now he has to struggle, and somewhere he has lost the will.

"Why do you have that, Pierce?" I ask him.

"For protection in the big bad city." He gives me the sly look, narrowing his eyes against the sun. He ties the red bandana around his head. "It's full of bad guys," he says. "Me among them."

"This isn't the big bad city. You really didn't have to bring that damn thing."

"I didn't like leaving it behind," he says. "This damn thing cost me half a week's pay." He raises the gun and points at a seagull posing on a rock. "Ka-boom, little guy."

"Pierce. Please."

Robbie wakes up as Pierce is aiming at another gull. "Jesus Christ," he says, and looks at me: *your friend, where did you get this jerk.*

"Relax," Pierce says. "It's not loaded. I'm not entirely crazy."

"Just don't aim that fucking thing at me," Robbie says.

Pierce aims it at him and says, "Ka-boom."

It's not a good place for swimming. The water is deep and clear green, but the rocks are brutal except around the bend, and over there the seaweed is thick and the water full of crabs. Robbie and I are used to our tame little backyard pond. Pierce grew up on the coast, but he hates the water, hates slimy things and things that crawl. We decide not to bother going in. We sit on the warm rocks, letting the water cool our feet, and eventually we get out the marijuana and smoke it in Pierce's little clay pipe. The sun gets lower in the sky. We will stay one more night, and then on Sunday morning the people from the marina will pick us up because the ferry doesn't run on Sundays. "But you'll have to wait until after church," they said, looking with distaste at Robbie's long hair, looking at me and imagining a drunken gang bang.

"People like that are what's wrong with this country," Pierce says. "People like that are what's running it, that's the scary part. You know what I mean? He looks at us and thinks: draft dodgers, punks, hippies. But catch that guy over in Vietnam charging up some hill with his M-1."

"You're not doing that either, buddy," Robbie points out amiably.

"I've been lucky," Pierce says. "But I'm not hiding out up here in America's vacationland doing the holier-than-thou routine in my madras-plaid Bermuda shorts. What was this guy doing when we were marching on Washington? Painting the boat, man. Shopping for new deck shoes."

I don't point out that what Pierce and Charlie did in Washington was get stoned in the Georgetown apartment of one of our old college pals. "Don't argue," I say. "I don't want anybody to argue."

Pierce puts his arm around me, and we sit looking at the sky just beginning to get pink over the town back on shore. The windows of the buildings shine gold, the hills behind them are purple. The only sound is the surf's gentle crash against the rocks, and us sucking on the pipe. I could stay there forever, much longer than the weekend. I think of telling Robbie I'd like to come up there with him and Dad next time, but it's too much trouble to talk. Then Pierce says, "Let's play a game."

Robbie asks, "What game?"

"Russian Roulette," says Pierce.

They get high, and they do it, and they make me watch. We sit on the lawn chairs. It is still very hot. The sky turns colors, the water turns black, and the mosquitoes come out. None of us notices the mosquitoes. We keep our eyes on the gun, which looks businesslike, lethal, and at the same time strangely unreal. Robbie and I used to have water pistols that looked like it. Pierce puts a bullet into the chamber and spins it. It's as if he has done this a dozen times: he is completely calm, he's laughing, he keeps telling me to calm down, not to worry, it's a game.

Robbie says, "It's no worse than driving up Route 1, Chris. In fact, your chances are probably better."

"Especially with all those drunken maniacs on the road yesterday," Pierce says.

"I hope you're not counting on me," I say. "You two can be as stupid as you want, but leave me out of it."

"No girls allowed, anyway," Pierce says. He holds up the gun and says, "I'll go first."

"Oh, do, by all means," Robbie says in an upper-crust accent. "After you, old man."

Even I laugh. Maybe we don't think he will really do it. Pierce sits with the gun in his hand, looking off at the horizon. For a moment I wonder if he's forgotten. Then, without warning, he raises the gun to his temple and pulls the trigger.

"Pierce!"

There must have been a click but I didn't hear it. He cradles the gun against his chest and smiles at me. "Christine, my dear. Please. A little dignity."

I put my hand over my mouth to keep myself from crying. The worst of it is the sky, the gorgeous sunset, rose and purple and gold. Robbie's head is outlined against it. I can't see his features. His skinny knees sticking out of his old cut-offs look like the knees of a little boy.

Pierce holds the gun out to Robbie. "Your turn, old fellow."

Robbie takes it, weighs it in his hand, examines it. I wish for the woman I met on my walk, or one of the old men—anyone—to appear from behind a rock and say something sane. *Any of you kids seen a dog? Have a few more of these plums. Do you have some matches we could borrow?*

I say, "Robbie, forget it."

"Calm down, Chris," he says. "A little dignity." He looks at Pierce.

Pierce says, "One if by land, two if by sea."

This makes no sense, but the two of them begin to cackle, loud hysterical laughing that sounds like gulls.

"You two are such jerks," I say. "I hate you when you're high. I hate you both."

They stop laughing. Pierce holds his cheeks and says, "Ooh."

Robbie reaches over and pats my knee, grinning. Then he sighs and says, "So what do I do? Just spin it?"

"Just give it a good one, old man."

"Right-o." He spins the chamber once, pauses, spins it again, and holds it to his head."

I cry out, "Don't!" and lunge toward him. He says, "Jesus, Chrissie," and lowers the gun. He looks toward Pierce, who leans forward to grab me.

"Leave him alone, Chrissie," he says. He holds my arms, draws me toward him, and pulls me down on his lap. "Now sit down like a good girl. Sit here with Uncle Pierce." We are awkward together in the flimsy chair. His arms are around me, clasped across my stomach. "There." He puts his lips against the back of my neck. "Chrissie Chrissie Chrissie," he says with a sigh.

Behind me, he seems to fall asleep, and I lie against him, watching my brother. He doesn't move. The .38 is in his lap. I think: we can just stay here, fall asleep, and then it will be morning, and this will be over. I also think about grabbing the gun away and tossing it as hard as I can into the depths of the sea.

But Pierce stirs and shifts position. He kisses the back of my neck. Desire goes through me, I want to turn and embrace him, pull him down on the sand and hold him. Distract him from this. *Maybe we think about it too much.* What does that mean? Is he thinking about it now?

He tightens his arms around me and says, "Okay, Rob."

Robbie has been aiming at a seagull, pretending to pull the trigger, like a nine-year-old with a capgun. I remember him as a nine-year-old with a capgun. He grins at us—I see the flash of his white teeth. "I'm high as a kite," he says, and puts the gun to his head. "Here goes. Next stop, Valhalla."

His finger on the trigger is outlined against the purple sky. Pierce holds me down. I scream out, "Robbie!"

But this time I hear the click.

~

"It's been like an illness that won't go away," I said to Orin.

"That's because it was unresolved. Because Pierce died offstage. And then it got complicated with your brother's death."

"Whatever."

"Maybe your having told me about it will help," Orin said. "All our talking."

"Maybe it will."

We had, in fact, discussed it endlessly. We'd gone over and over the Plover Island incidents—the trip there with Pierce and Robbie, and Robbie's suicide that next summer, eventually even my visitation from Robbie after I went to the island with Emile and Denis. I was unable to give Orin the details (the teapot, the cookies, the sunlight and shadow, and my screaming incoherence when the vision ended), about which I still felt a certain amount of shame and horror because of what happened afterward: I couldn't stop crying; I made a half-serious, messy attempt to cut my wrists, and Emile bundled me off to the Yale–New Haven psychiatric ward, telling me that he couldn't endure to see our son brought up by a woman in my condition. Worst of all was my acceptance of that. My seeing things, my breakdown, the bloody, farcical episode in the bathroom with the razor—for Emile, these added up to the opportunity, an excuse to be rid of me and get away to France and live the life he thought he deserved. I recognized the injustice, I even saw, vaguely, the possible damage that losing his mother could do to Denis. And still I accepted it. *You were self-destructive in many different ways, Christine,* Dr. Dalziel had said. *At that point, you lacked the energy to fight. But that is perfectly understandable, you need not blame yourself.* Understandable or not, these were things I still had trouble thinking about, and in talking to Orin I could be no more honest than to describe the vision of Robbie as a generalized sense of spiritual solace, as a vague but reassuring presence.

"Maybe this is what I came into your life for," Orin said. "To comfort you. To let you get this stuff off your chest."

"Maybe."

"What else can I do, Chris?" he asked me. "I want you to be happy—not haunted."

Haunted: what an exact word. "So be Pierce," I said. "*Really* Pierce. Then I can go back to square one and start my life over."

"I'll pretend to be Pierce. Tell me what to do."

I smiled at him. "Don't be silly."

"I want you to be happy."

"Orin, that's mad."

He shrugged. "Maybe it isn't. Maybe I'm Pierce, after all. Or maybe it *is* mad. So what?"

His eyes were dark, restless—that odd ocean-blue. How could that color not have haunted me all these years: Windsor Blue mixed with a little grey and a dab of Prussian Green.

"I want you to be happy," he said again. "Tell me what to do."

PART THREE

Plover Island

I always feel I am a traveler, going somewhere and to some
destination. If I tell myself that the somewhere and the
destination do not exist, that seems to me very reasonable
and likely enough.

Van Gogh, _Letters,_ Arles, August 1888

Chapter Eight

In bed together, we would play our game. There wasn't much to it: I'd call him Pierce, he would respond, and now and then I made him say: *it was you I loved, Chrissie—all those years, I loved you.*

Harmless.

We met every Saturday. I kept making my lame excuses to James: I need this, I need to look at paintings, I need the museums and the galleries, this is important to my work. I resurrected my old friend Beth, brought her back to New York from Taos, where she moved five years ago with Anthony, her sculptor-husband: we went gallery-hopping together, then we had dinner with Anthony and some of their artist-friends, and sometimes I stayed overnight with them at their place on East 57th.

James said this was fine with him, he was no longer jealous of my work and of my trips into the city, he was really glad I was being serious about painting again: the endless baskets of oranges had begun to worry him. I was still doing the self-portraits, though they were beginning to take another form, and they seemed to puzzle James—as, in fact, they puzzled me.

But he liked the big abstract landscapes I had been working on. I would cut huge sheets of 140-pound paper, soak and stretch them one by one, and paint from photographs. I photographed the Mill River as it wound down through East Rock, and from the top of East Rock I took shots of the city. I went out to Hugh and Helga's in the brisk spring weather and photographed abandoned fields, greening hills, and the tangles of forest and brush and rocks with their sudden, improbable burst of color. I painted for five, six hours at a time, I forgot to eat, I forgot who I was.

James was very polite with me, almost courtly. We didn't talk any more about getting married. Even when Hugh and Helga impulsively decided to have a wedding, we drank champagne and toasted them and when people asked us if we were going to be the next victims, we made jokes, not looking at each other. We watched a lot of television, rented movies to watch on the VCR we bought ourselves for Christmas. We seldom made love (we both talked about how tired we were), and we went out a lot with friends, or we walked down to Christopher Martin's hoping to run into someone we knew. We had lost the knack of being alone together and enjoying it. I disliked myself so much when I was with him that the only remedy was not to be with him. I am not a creature who lies and hides things (I said to myself). I am not a faithless woman. I am not a crazy, obsessive, deluded person.

George Drescher called me a couple of times, but I kept putting him off: he wouldn't like the new paintings, and I had a reluctance to put them into his hands. The little still lifes I did during the winter—oranges, baskets, flowers—yes, those could go, though George wouldn't want them. But I sent a bunch of paintings off to my rep, and most of them sold quickly. I sold six of the small things to one of Jimmy Luigi's steady customers, a doctor named Nathan who was redecorating his office. Another painting, a tentative stab at the landscapes I was working on, was bought by a wealthy Woodbridge woman who called me every year or so and asked to see what I had. I sent two of my Christmas paintings, framed, to my father for his birthday—views of the crumbling motel cottages. My mother called to say she hung them up in the study, he seemed to like them, but who could tell? There was a small show at a gallery run by a friend of mine, and she sold all three of the still lifes I gave her plus a couple of my failed self-portraits.

I used some of my earnings to buy spring clothes. Orin thought I looked good in primary colors: I bought a red dress, I bought black shoes with red stitching, I bought a black silk raincoat and a bright yellow scarf. On his advice, I started letting my hair grow.

George came up to New Haven to catch the show of German Expressionists at the Yale Art Gallery, and he stopped in to see James and me. He brought a woman called Lou-Ann. James offered to take us all over to Jimmy Luigi's for a pizza, but Lou-Ann smiled ruefully and patted her concave stomach. Instead, we had crackers and cheese and drinks in our living room. Lou-Ann accepted only plain seltzer. I was in jeans; she wore a white jersey dress that draped over her skinny bottom and was caught at the hip with the miniature ivory mask of a fierce warrior. She also wore a dangerous-looking copper arm bracelet. She was a decorator, and she sat on the edge of her chair looking around the room while we talked. "Charming," she said to me every once in a while. I imagined her living in a loft that was all chrome and glass and hard edges. "I like this place," she said. "It's quite perfect in its way. Really." We smiled at each other.

I should have disliked Lou-Ann but I didn't because her presence convinced James that there was nothing going on between George and me. I sense that George was disappointed in me, he was losing interest in showing my work at the Aurora, but we all trooped dutifully up to my studio, and he looked at the landscapes, and at the portraits from memory that I'd been doing—portraits whose subjects I couldn't identify. Pierce and Orin were there, of course, and my own face, and the faces of others, but the overall impression was of something else—certainly not of a portrait.

"What do you call these?" George asked without enthusiasm.

"I think of them as portrait-montages."

"I like some of the landscapes," he said, turning away. "The angle is sometimes odd, I'm not sure what you're getting at, but I like the colors. Gutsy. What's this? A seascape?"

It was another of the portrait-montages: What might have been there, underneath the faces, was Plover Island. "Sort of, I guess."

"The landscapes are promising," George said. "You've given up on the self-portraits?"

"Well, lately I'm just doing these," I told him.

We all stood quietly, looking. George was gloomy. Lou-Ann ran her hand along the back of a chair, picked up one of my old blue Mason jars, looked dubiously at Ruby asleep amid the junk on the table.

James's face was serene. *Not George* I imagined him thinking. Eventually, he would wonder: *Who, then? What?* But for the moment he was at peace.

"Well, stay in touch," George said, and Lou-Ann at the front door said, "This is such a dear little place." She patted the wildly carved mahogany commode in the front hall that was our pride and joy. We outbid a dozen gimlet-eyed dealers for it at an auction in Greenwich. "You really do have an eye for this sort of thing," Lou-Ann said.

"Gee, thanks," I said to her. James shook George's hand much too heartily and said, "Great to see you both! Come again!"

James didn't immediately get beyond the idea that it wasn't George. After George's visit, he cheered up a lot. The next Sunday afternoon, when he picked me up at the station, he wanted to know everything: How was Beth? Where did we go? Where did we eat— anyplace good? Somebody had told him about a video-performance artist at the Guggenheim: had I seen that yet? If I could have kept lying, all would have been well, but he was so sweet and supportive that I lost the will to lie to him. I withdrew, I dismissed his questions, I developed headaches and cramps when he reached for me in bed, I told him I was too tired to talk and he wouldn't be interested anyway. He was puzzled, and then he realized that there was a simple explanation. I saw his attitude change from hurt to hostility to sorrow. He knew, and I knew he knew, and he knew I knew he knew, etc. But neither of us said a word.

It saddened me, the mess my life with James was becoming, but it was also, in a sense, unreal to me. There were only two real things in my life: my painting and Pierce.

Pierce: Orin—yes, I knew, I never stopped knowing that Orin wasn't "really" Pierce. And yet he was, of course. By which I mean that my life had expanded to include a new definition of "real." What was real was what I said was real. Like a play: more real, more intense than life. Orin and I were playwright, actor, audience. It was an extraordinary theatrical event: four stars, two thumbs up, and best of all the play would never end.

He was in love with me. He told me that as Pierce (in bed) and as Orin (in the Metro, at Clarissa's, walking through Central Park on a Saturday afternoon where I thought I saw Silvie at every turn but didn't care anymore). He said he would do anything, play any game, tell any wacko lie, to make me happy, to keep these Saturdays and Sundays in his life.

I wondered at this, and at his attraction to me. The truth was that I was forty-four and thickening around the middle, my gums were receding, my hair wasn't gray but it had no gloss. Orin and I were almost exactly the same age, but young women gave him the eye on the street and men hardly glanced at me. Besides, I was already living with someone, I was obviously pretty eccentric (to put it nicely), and I made bizarre demands on him. Yet Orin said he loved me. He met my train, and we went instantly to bed. Later, we went out, ate dinner, listened to music in one of he quiet jazz clubs he liked, went back to his place and maybe made love again, slept late, ate brunch together, and I was back on the 2:00 train to New Haven. I always brought a book with me, but I never read: I would remember the way he turned to me in bed, his hands on my body waking me up on Sunday morning, the clean line of his backbone, his hard freckled shoulders.

I knew he was not Pierce. Pierce had died in New Mexico more than twenty years ago. This was Orin Pierce of Sarasota, Florida. I could verify this easily, but I didn't. What I did was look constantly for traces of Pierce. His face, his speech, his mannerisms—I never stopped weighing and analyzing. It gave me pleasure, whether I found Orin there or Pierce.

I also inspected his apartment: the co-op on East 57th Street, where for a while I lodged Beth and Anthony and the studio they shared, their tiny guest room, their Yorkshire terrier named Princess Di. The reality was two large rooms and a kitchenette in a bland brick building where Orin had lived for ten years. The place was neat and spare and plain—sturdy modern furniture, museum posters on the walls.

For several weeks, the inspection of Orin's apartment was my passion. He took long showers, and while he was in the bathroom on Sunday mornings, I searched. I was very quiet, very careful. I was reminded of playing pick-up sticks: always be aware of what's under things, what's on top of them, what holds them up, what could fall. And I was thorough. I stood in the middle of each room and thought: where? what? how? I became clever at opening things silently, at disarranging nothing. With a pair of thin lightweight gloves I could work for the police, or the FBI.

There was not much:

dresser drawers (underwear, sweaters, socks, condoms);

bedroom closet (four suits, a dozen shirts, jackets and pants, a pair of sneakers, shoes);

hall closet (camelhair topcoat, trench coat, scarves, down jacket from Lands' End, hiking boots, empty suitcase in the back);

kitchen cupboards (All-Bran, canned tuna, spaghetti, Newman's Own marinara sauce, Progresso lentil soup);

refrigerator (milk, beer, celery, butter, a plastic bag of almonds, mayonnaise, a dessicated onion wrapped in plastic, and frozen spinach and half a loaf of French bread in the freezer);

linen closet (sheets, toilet paper, an extra blanket, a sheep-shaped hot water bottle with a fluffy cover);

broom closet (broom, Raid, shoe polish, carpet sweeper);

bookcase (mysteries, spy novels, a few classics—*War and Peace, Great Expectations, Jude the Obscure,* a dictionary, *Out of Africa,* letters of E.B. White, *The Soul of a New Machine, Less Than Zero*—all in paperback, none inscribed, underlined, or annotated, including a copy of Van Gogh's *Letters* that made my heart jump until I saw that it was new-looking, the spine not even broken);

medicine cabinet, which I inspected after my own shower with the water in the sink running hard (generic aspirin, scissors, Ban, Aqua-Fresh, Dr. Scholl's Athlete's Foot Powder, and a prescription bottle of antibiotics dating back two years—two capsules left);

record shelf (heavy on jazz piano, Vivaldi, and Ella Fitzgerald).

That was all, really. Odds and ends: tape and string, scissors, pens, plastic wrap, telephone (no book of phone numbers), dishes and silverware and pans, salt shakers, paper napkins—oh, the usual, nothing even slightly interesting, nothing that said one word about Orin Pierce except that he was a tidy man with simple tastes—or a man who, perhaps, wished to reveal nothing about himself.

It was almost as if the apartment were a particularly brilliant stage set, created as part of the characterization of the star in a one-man show called Orin Pierce—the kind of set the audience applauds when the lights come up. So perfect! So authentic! Right down to the honestly dog-eared books, the mud clinging to the hiking boots, the odd laundry or bookstore receipt in the pockets of his jackets, the handle of the suitcase found with a luggage ticket from Lambert Airport in St. Louis to Kennedy Airport in New York. What was missing: bank statements, cancelled checks, tax information, bills. I assumed he kept all that in his office or with his accountant. Also photographs, personal letters, junk, quirks, eccentricities—but of course none of this was necessary for the creation of this particular character, who was composed of the memories, quirks, and eccentricities of someone else: me.

It would not be inaccurate to say that after my careful inspection of Orin Pierce's apartment, he was more of an enigma to me than ever. And yet I willingly, gladly let him assume a major role in my life. I didn't know if I loved him or not. I never told him I did, though I was haunted by what he once said, that no one had ever loved him the way I loved Pierce. Certainly, I had a craving to be with him that resembled love. When I was not with him, I thought of him: this also resembled love.

In a sense, although we had our games when I called him by Pierce's name, he was taking the place of Pierce in my life. As time went by, I found that I no longer thought of the real Pierce, the old Pierce—not even the way I did in the days before I met Orin, when I used to think of Pierce so much: "often, but a little at a time," as Swann's father thought of his dead wife. I was finding that when I tried to bring Pierce into my mind, it was Orin's face that I saw, his voice I heard. This made me sad, but I didn't fight it, and that also seemed to me a sign of love.

When I explored Orin's apartment, or tried to put together what I knew about him, my motive was not so much, any longer, to prove that he was or wasn't either Pierce *redux* or Orin Pierce of Sarasota, but to solve the mystery of who he was. Orin never talked about his past: childhood, school, old loves, dashed hopes, struggles to make it in the world—all of this was missing from his conversation. It was as if he began to exist the day we met. He was still telling me I should check him out: birth certificates, school records, old friends—let's fly down to Florida and visit his mother, let's go to St. Louis and see his friend Jake Thomas. Or I should investigate Pierce's death, get in touch with Pierce's family. We could go to New Mexico together for a vacation; we could stay in a hacienda he knew in Chimayo, and we could look up police records of the accident, the investigation, the way the bodies were identified.

This was no longer what interested me. It was he who was curious about Pierce; what I was interested in was Orin. Not just the facts— it was the essence I wanted, the truth, the reality that wasn't revealed on a birth certificate or an employment record. I wanted to know him as I knew James. "Tell me who you are," I demanded of him—in the Metro, across the breakfast table, in bed—but invariably he pretended not to understand. He would turn the conversation to something impersonal, entertain me with stories about the people he met in his work and on the landmarks committee, talk about what he read in the newspaper. He joked, teased me and made me laugh, or he would say nothing at all and lower his mouth to my breasts.

Sometimes I suspected that his place on 57th Street was a stripped-down duplicate of wherever he really lived. I wondered if the walls of his other home were lined with photographs (of me? of Charlie? of his professor-parents?). I wondered if the drawers there were stuffed with letters instead of neat, unused piles of notepads and envelopes, if the books on the shelves were underlined and scribbled in and branded with bookplates bearing his name.

Tell me who you are. He kept slipping out of my grasp, and it occurred to me one day that this was precisely what Pierce used to do.

Chapter Nine

Out of the blue, I got a phone call from Alison Kaye asking me if I wanted to have lunch with her.

"I ran into Orin the other day," she said. "He was telling me about you, and I remembered our phone conversation that time. Do you want to get together?"

My first thought was that she wanted to sell me something. I was trying to remember what she did, what Haver & Schmidt was. Did I ever know?

I couldn't think how to get out of it, so I said yes, of course, we could have lunch any time. As we talked, I realized I didn't want to get out of it, even if she was trying to sell me something. Alison Kaye had become one of the people I associated with what I thought of as "the whole Pierce thing"—the part of my life that began with her sitting next to me on the train. She was someone who regularly ran into Orin, who seemed to know him pretty well; possibly, she could tell me something useful, though I was hard pressed to imagine what that could be.

"I think we'll have a lot to talk about," she said. "I'm really looking forward to it."

We picked a day—the next Thursday. I decided to have lunch with her and then check out the folk art exhibit at the Whitney. I told James I was going to New York during the week to meet a friend of Beth's who also worked in watercolor. James said, "Fine," as he always did.

Raymond took me aside one night at Jimmy Luigi's and asked, "Is something bugging our boy James?" and I responded, looking surprised, "Not that I know of." I had the feeling that Raymond wasn't fooled. He had also commented, more than once, that he didn't see me around much lately, a statement to which I could give no convincing reply. *I've been busy* elicited a skeptical grin.

I called Orin and told him I was having lunch with Alison.

He seemed momentarily disconcerted. "Oh—right—I ran into her," he said. "We were talking about you."

"What does she do? Does she want to sell me something? I mean—why would she want to see me?"

Orin said, "Alison doesn't sell anything you could possibly be interested in," and laughed. For a moment I wondered if Alison was a high-level call girl or a crack dealer. He said, "Don't worry—you're not in for another real estate spiel. But hey—you're sure you're not in the market? I've got a nice little place in Gramercy Park, just what you're looking for, and I'm sure I can work out some creative financing for you. It needs a little work, but it would be perfect for an artistic-type lady like you."

This was one of our jokes—Orin doing his sleazeball-realtor routine. It was designed to change the subject, but when I pressed him, what he told me about Alison was perfectly innocent: she designed custom software configurations for small business. She was one of the best in her field. Orin said, "She did some incredible work for us here at Parker. What makes her so good is that she knows the hardware, too, inside and out. She used to be at Intel, actually. She was in hardware for years."

This meant very little to me: I couldn't help thinking of hardware as bad and software as good—sharp-edged tools and missile parts versus a pile of wool freshly sheared from a sheep, a divan piled high with cushions. I knew this was stupid, I even knew generally what these words really meant. There was no way to live in the world and not know such things, though I didn't have a computer. I kept the books for Jimmy Luigi's with the help of an adding machine and huge pebbled black ledgers that suggested *Bleak House* and *Bartleby the Scrivener*. James special-ordered them from a stationery store in Boston. He would probably have liked it if he'd caught me making entries with a quill pen. Most of his friends in the business had succumbed, but James scorned the idea of using a computer for the simple operations necessary to running a pizza parlor: computers represented the world he gave up in order to make the best pizza in New Haven. When computer salesmen called, which for some reason they regularly did, James said, "The only machine I need for making pizza is a brick oven, thanks."

I asked Orin why on earth Alison could possibly want to have lunch with me. He said it wasn't because she wanted anything from me—she was just a nice, friendly person who was intrigued by the situation.

"The situation?" I could see why he was trying to change the subject. "What situation? Ours? You told her about it?"

"Well, it was her Filo-Fax that brought us together. I thought she deserved to know."

I felt the blood rush to my face. "Oh, God, Orin. Now she knows I lied to her on the phone. What in hell is she thinking?"

"She's thinking it's great." He was cheerful, but there was a note of worry in his voice, and he added quickly, "She thinks you're really nice, and she's interested in this just as—I don't know—" He faltered again. "Human nature. I mean, this is *interesting*."

"How much did you tell her?"

"Not much, obviously. Though she knows we're seeing each other. I just told her that thanks to her, I've met a wonderful woman that I'm crazy about. She thought it made a great story." He paused, said, "Chris? You're not offended, are you? I'm sorry. Really—I didn't think. I ran into Alison at a cocktail thing, and we just got talking. Do you mind?"

When I wasn't with him, I constantly imagined him in a New York that was infinitely more racy and glamorous than the city he showed me. I imagined him meeting young and beautiful women at cocktail things and having conversations about software. I imagined them in his bed, their red lips on his skin, their lacquered fingernails on his spine. Their flesh was young and firm, they had perfect legs. I hated these thoughts: they were not thoughts I had ever considered myself capable of having. In spite of my troubles with Emile, my lonely times, my various failures with men, I was never that kind of woman—insecure, dependent on men's approval. I'd seen my friends weeping over men, waiting by the phone, giving in to jealous fantasies, berating themselves for bad complexions or small breasts or big feet. Bridget was the worst: she spent years in thrall to a really dreadful man who treated her like dirt. I used to hold her hands and pat her shoulder and try to either talk her out of it or console her. I understood her miseries, but I didn't actually experience these feelings myself. I considered myself lucky that though I liked men I could shrug them off when necessary. Even Emile. It was Denis I missed, the loss of Denis I reproached myself with.

Even Pierce. I loved Pierce the way I loved—what? The pond out behind our house. The sun. The idea of the dark heart of the jungle, with its tigers and elephants. I knew that I would never have Pierce, and that though he never quite managed to make it with me, he made it with countless other women. But that was never what I tortured myself with.

I used to be a different person: I was myself, I didn't wear leather shoes, I never told lies, I didn't wear eyeshadow, I didn't spend money on clothes, I didn't speculate about the skin of younger women, Raymond didn't look at me with amused distrust. *I was doing well:* I almost said that to Orin on the phone. *I was doing so well and now I'm coming apart, I'm crumbling, I'm breaking down, I don't know who I am, I'm losing all my hardware, I'm becoming a pile of software, I'm a mess.*

"Christine? Do you mind?"

"I don't know, Orin."

"I certainly didn't tell her anything much. Just the basic facts, that my name is the same as someone you used to know, and you wondered if I was the same guy, and you decided to look me up. And then we fell for each other."

"That's all?"

"Christine—what do you think? Jesus."

I said, "I'm sorry. It just strikes me as so odd that she wants to have lunch with me."

He said, "You have a way of finding the most ordinary things odd and the oddest things ordinary."

"I do? Is that true? Is that my problem?" How simple: I just had to turn a switch.

"It's not a problem, it's one of your lovable little quirks," he said, and then, "I miss you. Am I going to get to see you next week after your lunch with Alison?"

"Can you?"

"Thursday night? I can't imagine why not. Can you stay with me? Or do you have to go home to the white-clam king of Connecticut?"

"I don't know, let me think." I hated it when he made fun of James, whom he insisted on considering a ludicrous figure. I didn't tell him about James's pigtail, which was getting quite long.

"In fact, why don't you just stay until the weekend? I'll have to work, but maybe you could go to museums or something, and I'll try to keep my schedule to a minimum. We'll have the nights."

Oh God, it was tempting. I thought of James, and hated myself— Orin's ridicule always made me feel tender toward James. But I knew that it would be a relief to be away from him and from the nothingness that was growing between us.

"Do it, Chris. Please. What a time we'll have."

"I'll have to think about it. Sometimes I work on Thursday nights."

"What—slinging oregano?"

"Yes, slinging oregano. Orin—stop it."

"I'm sorry," he said. "I just want to see you so badly."

～

Alison was wearing another suit, a lightweight blue wool with a straight skirt and an open-neck blouse. I wore my new red dress. We met at Chez Duroc—*Chez D*—a pretty little French restaurant just off Madison Avenue.

"This must seem strange to you," she said immediately. She looked quizzically at me over her menu. She was not quite as pretty as I remembered her, or as young, but she was still very attractive: a sharp-nosed face, bright lipstick, the thick, perfectly-streaked hair. "That I wanted us to meet for lunch."

I started to say something polite, and then I decided to be honest. "Yes, I guess it did—a little."

"But I remembered our phone call, and you seemed so nice—I mean, I liked you on the phone." She smiled at me. "And then Orin told me this amazing story, and I thought: I have to meet this woman! I love it when things are extravagant, larger than life. Don't you? It's such a romantic story."

"Is it?"

"Of course!"

She beamed at me. I figured out that she was about thirty-six. Her make-up was perfect; there was a pearly blue line between the edge of her lower lid and her eyelashes; each eyelash was pristinely stiff with mascara; her cheekbones were plum-colored fading to the same pink as her lipstick. Her eyes were so brilliantly green she must have worn tinted contact lenses.

"And Orin is such a dear," Alison went on. "I thought, well, I'll have lunch with Christine, and then the four of us can get together for dinner some night—I'll bring Roger—my fiancé. Did Orin mention Roger to you?" I shook my head. "Oh, you'll love Roger. I really want to do this soon. But for the moment, let's order and get that over with, and then we can really talk. I want to know everything!"

Alison ate a lot—she said she had to because she had low blood sugar—and she ordered a bottle of wine that she kept sloshing into our glasses. She was not what I expected: from her appearance, her absorbed efficiency that day on the train, the incredible schedule I glimpsed in her Filo-Fax. I had imagined her as brisk, cold, overbearing—definitely a hardware kind of person—not someone I would feel comfortable with. But though her self-confidence was staggering, she was relaxed and friendly. She said she needed a long lunch hour to unwind from the morning and fortify herself for the afternoon and evening.

"All the guys I know like to brag that they work hard and they play hard," she said, and made a face. "As if those are virtues. I think it sounds desperate and pathetic—not the working hard part, I like to work hard, I thrive on it—up to a point, of course. But playing hard—isn't that sad? Although what it comes down to with them is women and booze." She grinned; her teeth were what you'd expect. "But I like to enjoy myself. You know what I mean?" She held up a shrimp speared on the end of her fork. "I believe in pleasure."

Alison also believed in talking—very fast, very intimately. She told me about her childhood and asked about mine, which fascinated her: Jamesville High, and parents who ran a motel in the country. She had never heard anything like that before "My God," she said. "A real high school with cheerleaders and car washes and an honor roll." She went to the Dalton School in Manhattan. I told her that the only Dalton girl I knew at Oberlin had a nervous breakdown during Orientation Week.

"Exactly," Alison said with triumph. "See what I mean?"

I wasn't sure I did. I went to Jamesville High and spent three months in a psychiatric ward making baskets.

I didn't tell her that, though our conversation quickly got to the point where we could confess anything to each other. She told me about her parents' noisy drunken cocktail parties when she used to sit weeping in terror in the kitchen with the maid; I told her that I always hated the way my parents were with the motel guests (my mother so servile, my father so brusque); we talked about our hair; I told her some things about Emile, and about Denis and Yale; she told me the trouble she'd had getting over her abortion; I told her about George Drescher's gallery; she told me about going to Argentina to design a system for the largest beef cattle ranch in the world; I told her about Jimmy Luigi's; she told me about her sister who got a tattoo of a naked man on her left bicep; I asked her about Roger; she asked me about being a clam-eating vegetarian.

We went on and on: we were becoming friends, and our conversation quickened with the consciousness of that fact. I felt the afternoon getting away from me while I galloped into a closeness to Alison that I wasn't prepared for; I could sense that I was on the verge of revealing things I didn't really want to say to anyone. I could understand why Orin told her so much about us: she was impossible to resist.

This was something that happened to me more often with women than with men, though it was what drew James and me together: the immediate, unmistakable sense of rightness, of comfort and trust. Talking to Alison, I thought of the way that block on Chapel Street between Jimmy Luigi's and Claire's would always bear the light of James's first goodness to me, the winter day he volunteered Rosie and Ruby and then took me out for herb tea and coffee cake.

I had missed that intimacy. James and I had lost it, and I didn't have it with Orin—not like this, not so purely. We were happy in each other's company; he was gregarious and entertaining, and he listened to whatever I wanted to tell him. But I was aware that we didn't always get through to each other, that sometimes I couldn't judge his reactions to my words, that he seemed to be withholding things from me. There were times when I knew things he never would, or when he seemed urgently attuned to what eluded me completely. These small lapses were, in a way, the aspects of Orin that recalled Pierce to me most vividly—the failures to connect, the momentary lack of symmetry, the tiny instances of frustration. None of this had anything to do with love, and certainly not with passion. Pierce and I had been best friends; and in bed, Orin and I understood each other perfectly.

Alison polished off her shrimp, ate all the bread and butter, and helped me finish my vol-au-vent with spring vegetables. She told me about her new apartment and the reproduction William Morris wallpaper she had chosen for the dining room. We found that we shared a taste for the most extreme examples of Victorian furniture, and she wanted to know all the details about the auction where James and I found the flamboyant mahogany commode. She also liked Stickley, and she was interested in early twentieth century oak, the good stuff, and she wanted to hear all about my watercolors, she'd love a watercolor for her dining room, something strong that wouldn't be overpowered by all the pattern.

When I looked at my watch, I saw that we had been at lunch for nearly two hours. What happened to the busy yuppie who thrived on hard work? How long could a long lunch hour be? Didn't she say she had appointments? And wasn't I going to go to the Whitney?

As if she had read my mind, Alison said, "I hope you're not in any particular hurry. I don't have an appointment until four, and then I'm flying to D.C. on the red-eye. I just finished a huge, complicated, pricey and *extremely boring* job." She grinned—proud of herself and trying not to show it. "So I told myself I'm just going to chill out for a day—you know? Spend some time away from those bloody machines!"

The restaurant had emptied out, our table by the window was a little oasis of clanking silverware. The waiter was hovering, he wanted us to leave, but we ordered more coffee, and Alison insisted that we have dessert. I gave the waiter a sheepish smile, but Alison said, "Frank, you don't mind if we stay, do you? Can you keep pouring coffee into us for a while?" Frank agreed, of course; he seemed delighted, whether he was or not. This was a way of life I didn't yet understand: the unapologetic life, the life of privilege, the life in which friendship, talk, intimacy—pleasure—were more important than the convenience of some waiter—the life led by the glamorous people who besieged Orin when I wasn't around.

"Isn't this wonderful?" Alison grinned at me. She didn't look glamorous. Her lipstick was gone, her upper lip was greasy, she had had too much wine. But somehow she managed to continue to look like what she was: a busy professional woman, one of the best in her field. "Aren't we having fun?" she asked me. "I'm awfully glad I took the plunge and called you."

"I thought you wanted to sell me something," I confessed. "I had no idea what Haver & Schmidt was."

She got the giggles at this, and imagined designing a system for what she called the watercolor biz. But in spite of my liking for Alison, in spite of our instant rapport, I kept wondering why she did, in fact, telephone me and invite me to lunch.

And then, over our second coffees, the conversation turned to Orin. She and Orin had been friends for ages, Alison said—when pressed, she guessed about five years. She met him through Roger, before she and Roger got engaged, when Roger was involved with a friend of hers. Orin and Roger did a lot of work together—Roger was in real estate law as well as taxes—and when she set up the new installations for Parker Properties she worked pretty closely with Orin and really got to know him.

"But it's your friend Pierce who interests me," Alison said. "Orin is such a mystery man. The Scarlet Pimpernel. It really intrigues me that you thought he might be someone else." She looked at me brightly. "You know?"

"It was just a crazy idea of mine," I said.

She looked disappointed. "You don't think so anymore?"

"It's too impossible."

Alison toyed with her spoon. She peered at her face in it, frowning. "Well, I don't see how you can just *give up* on it," she said. "It does have a certain plausibility." She put down the spoon and looked at me. "I mean, he really could be this guy Pierce," she said. "Orin. He could be the guy you lost twenty years ago, Christine. The guy you thought was dead. Couldn't he?"

I was unable to respond. We sat there looking at each other, and then I dropped my eyes to my plate and squeezed my hands together in my lap. It had been starting to be over, and now it was beginning again, and I thought to myself: *of course.* This is not crazy. It makes the most perfect sense, as if I have been working at cleaning an old canvas, delicately removing layers of paint to expose different realities until I reach, finally, not the blank white canvas I thought was the end but something below even that, something infinitely richer than I could have anticipated.

What was crazy was not to trust my instincts. The moment I saw him, I thought: *Pierce. Yes. Of course.* And then I drove it away, I had been doing what I could to drive it away ever since.

The old longing returned: for Pierce, my Pierce, who played the guitar and sang the blues, who bought me a wind-up penguin and quoted from Van Gogh's letters—my dearest friend, whom I would miss until I died.

I raised my eyes at last and looked at Alison. She had been finishing her pastry, an apricot tarte, snatching the food off her fork with quick little bites, watching me across the table while I struggled with what she said. "I hope I didn't open some can of worms that's none of my business," she said. "Sometimes I get carried away."

She looked somehow voracious, but her voice was kind, and she seemed genuinely concerned. I wondered if she was the sort of person who fed on other people's lives because her own was unsatisfactory. I wondered briefly about Roger, her fiancé—the tax and real estate lawyer who spent years traveling in India, toyed with the idea of entering a monastery, and now was a workaholic obsessed with being made partner in the firm where he worked. Roger had to sleep with a night light, Alison told me.

"Christine?" She pushed away her plate and reached across the table briefly to touch my arm, a gesture that reminded me of Orin. "Should I apologize? I do apologize. Okay?"

I shook my head. "I just—I thought I'd finally settled all this in my mind, I thought I had gotten to the point—slowly, and with great difficulty gotten to the point where I had eliminated Pierce, all that madness, and it was just Orin, it was just having an affair with someone. I thought that was complicated enough."

"Oh God." Her eyes blazed with sympathy. "I really don't want to upset you. I don't have anything to go on, it's just a feeling I had the whole time I was talking to Orin, when he was telling me about this—that there could be something else behind everything he was saying. You know what I mean?" She signaled to Frank for more coffee. "And, of course, you know that Orin used to be an actor."

My heart gave a lurch. "He never told me that." I remembered, though, what she said to me on the phone that day: *he's a real con man,* her voice full of laughter.

"Now that is really odd," Alison said, leaning forward, nodding her head, tapping the table in front of her with one finger, as if that was where the oddness lay. "Because he was quite good, and he was fairly well known in St. Louis. There's a little repertory theater there. He was one of their shining lights."

"You mean he was a professional?" I was amazed, and then I wasn't. Since the moment I met him, I had thought of him as an actor—a natural actor, a mimic, all part of his personality, his ability to entertain. *A real con man. Something else behind everything he's saying.* "I can't believe he wouldn't tell me that."

Frank approached and poured coffee. Alison turned her head and smiled vaguely in his direction but kept her sympathetic eyes on my face. "It is a bit weird," she said.

"Unless Orin Pierce is indeed Orin Pierce." I spoke the words reluctantly, wearily. Suddenly what I wanted to do was take a cab over to Silvie's, borrow her guest room and go to sleep.

"And he's been in hiding all these years?" asked Alison. "But hiding from what? And why emerge now? How can you be in hiding and be a professional actor at the same time? And who died in New Mexico? And if you hadn't found him, would he have found you?" She dumped sugar into her coffee and said, "Actually, the Pierce story answers a lot of questions I've always had about Orin. He's a very elusive guy—have you noticed that? What do you know about his past? And Roger agrees with me. If Orin doesn't want you to know something, you damn well don't know it. Am I right?"

She was right. And yet he was always trying to get me to check his background, send for his birth certificate, meet his old friends. I told this to Alison and she dismissed it. "He could easily have certain things programmed and ready to go. An old lady down in Florida, various forged papers—who knows? Actor pals. What I'd do if I were you is check something he can't fix, some detail that's official—I don't know—school records or something. One of these things he keeps daring you to check. Take him up on it. It's worth a try—you might learn something interesting."

She had that Nancy Drew look in her eyes—the voraciousness I'd seen before. She was beginning to irritate me. I started to say something, but she forged ahead. "The question we keep coming back to is *why?*" She shrugged. "It could be a lot of things. Maybe he murdered someone. Or drove someone to his death."

I was suddenly cold: a chill fell over our table, our coffee cups, the silver pitcher of cream and the remains of dessert. Orin had said exactly those words once—or nearly. In the Metro that first day? Yes—and then we had talked about movies, what would happen if this were a movie. I forced myself to pick up my water glass and drink from it. My hand didn't tremble. And yet the movie had become *Gaslight*—Alison and Orin combining to drive me crazy.

I knew, of course, that this explanation was as far-fetched as any of them, I had read enough murder mysteries to understand the importance of motive. Sheer malice wasn't enough, or the pleasures of torture for its own sake. Money had to be involved, or love, or revenge, or madness. None of these seemed to provide a coherent explanation.

Alison was staring into her coffee cup with frowning concentration. "Or maybe he just wanted to shake off his old life and come out of hiding—start over. Like what's-her-name, the Weatherwoman."

"Why did you say that?" I asked her suddenly. "About driving someone to his death?" I didn't wait for an answer. Unable to stop myself, I went on. "Because for years I blamed Pierce for my brother's suicide."

Alison looked confused, and I realized that during our long conversation I had barely mentioned Robbie's name. "My brother Robbie shot himself with Pierce's gun. He was twenty years old. This was after Pierce was dead, but I used to be afraid Pierce had something to do with it. I worried about it for years."

My head was beginning to ache: too much wine, too much food, too much late-afternoon sunlight glaring in at our table by the window. Too much thinking about the unthinkable in its various guises. *I hereby exonerate Pierce from any and all wrongdoing:* I could hear Robbie saying those words, I could see the shadows move across his face until he disappeared back into them. I could hear myself screaming until Emile came.

"I don't mean that it's something we need to talk about," I told Alison. My voice was strained and breathless. The headache escalated. "It was just what you said—about someone being driven to his death—I wondered if it really meant anything or if you were just—" I made a vague gesture. "Just nattering on. Just playing Miss Marple."

She was shocked. She said, "God, Chris, I certainly didn't mean that, I didn't mean anything at all, it was movie talk, I don't think there's anything *sinister* going on."

"Orin suggested that same thing. That Pierce murdered someone, or—" I kept getting confused. Did Orin really say this? Because if Pierce was alive Orin was talking about himself: every speculation about Pierce could be a truth. "You see—"

I stopped again. What exactly did I want to say? Whatever had been lurking beneath it all since the moment Alison sat down next to me on the train. This was suddenly clear to me. "If Orin is really Pierce, if Pierce has been alive all these years, then it's horrible, it's evil, it's—I mean the deception, the betrayal of so much." What I was really thinking of was Robbie, but I didn't want to talk about Robbie anymore. I went on. "Even the idea that someone could change so much, or that you don't really know someone who's close to you."

Alison nodded. "It's scary."

There was a silence. I saw Orin again in his office: the White Rabbit, the balding man in the three-piece suit polishing his spectacles. Could Pierce really have come to this? I said, "But if he's not Pierce, then nothing in the world makes any sense." The words shocked me even as I spoke them: I hadn't known I believed this, that my endless vacillating had ended in this blunt reality. And yet, *Of course,* was the first thing I had thought. *Yes.*

"It's certainly a bizarre coincidence," Alison said. "And I suppose that has to be the truth—either that, or we live in a world where you have to decide between evil and absurdity." We sat looking at each other. I had no way of knowing how serious she was, or how much of this conversation was like a game to her—fun, like racquetball or Trivial Pursuit. She leaned forward and said, "Oh come on, Christine—you should just check him out. Make some phone calls. I'm so *curious!*"

"Alison. Please." I could feel tears behind my eyes, and I willed them not to spill over. "At this point, I just wish it would leave me alone," I told her. "I wish I could go back to the way I was. I wish I weren't sitting in this restaurant being so *miserable.*"

I heard my voice rise. Alison looked alarmed. She ran her hand back through her hair; her hair fell perfectly back into place, but her face was troubled: flushed slightly, it showed lines, and she looked her age. "Oh, Christine, forgive me. I've gotten all wrapped up in this idea. It would explain so much about Orin. But I'm probably wrong. And I for sure don't want to upset you. I'm sorry, let's drop it."

But I knew that what I needed was to continue. I needed to know the truth, if there was any more truth to be known. I took a deep breath. "I'd like to talk about it a little more, actually," I said. "Unless you're in a hurry."

She shrugged and shook her head. "I think you do need to talk about it, Christine. And I'm sorry to be such a voyeur, but—" She smiled a little, apologetically. "I'm fascinated, I have to admit it. I mean, nothing this interesting ever happens to *me.*"

"Well, why would he use his own name?" I asked abruptly. I seized on this detail because it was baffling but concrete; it was the sort of puzzle Nancy Drew and Miss Marple might discuss profitably together over their tea. "You say he was well-known as an actor in St. Louis," I pointed out. "Why wouldn't he use a stage name?"

"Easier." Her eyes were bright; she liked it, I could see, that the conversation was becoming normal again: *two women gossiping in a restaurant.* "He wouldn't have to forge anything. But I think the main thing is that it introduces an element of risk—of chance. Have you ever been to the track with Orin? He's really into it—the whole gambling thing. Get him to take you to Belmont sometime."

"That answers my next question, I suppose."

"What was your next question?"

"Why would he get involved with me?"

"The risk?" She smiled again. "Maybe—aside from the fact that he seems to be genuinely crazy about you." I didn't smile back. She said, "And then there's the idea that if he's ready to come out of hiding you'd be the one he'd trust."

"But I'm the one who found *him*," I pointed out. "It was sheer chance, my sitting next to you on the train, and then following it up, calling you, calling him." I didn't know Pierce at all, as it turned out: how could he know me so well? How could he know I would *act?* Pierce, who once told me I lacked passion. I added, "At least, I assume it was chance. Who knows?" I felt slightly ridiculous, but I had to say it. And what did I have to lose? I had already shown Alison all my worst, craziest sides. "I mean, you and Orin are friends, you know him pretty well, and if there's some sort of deception going on—"

She put down her cup, suddenly, and folded her hands together, elbows on the table. She was still smiling, but incredulously, with a touch of coolness, eyes wide: the Comtesse d'Haussonville. "Christine," she said. "What on earth is going through your mind?"

This time, the tears spilled over—a familiar feeling, not entirely unpleasant. "I keep trying to stay rational," I told her. "I know I have a tendency to go off the deep end. But I do know this isn't some cheap melodramatic movie, Alison," I said. "I do know you aren't collaborating with Orin in some plot to drive me crazy. When I'm myself, I know that. This is life, it's not a movie or an Agatha Christie novel, and life doesn't work that way, life isn't so—*interesting,* as you say. So wacky. Whatever. This is *National Enquirer* stuff and everyone knows that's invented by a staff of maniacs in Jersey City." I laughed a little, shakily. I didn't look at Alison. I had no idea how she was reacting to this. I wiped my eyes on my napkin. The napkin was a deep rose madder, the color of Alison's blusher, and my tears left blotches like red wine stains. I went on, I couldn't stop talking. "And yet this *is* driving me crazy," I told her. "I want so much for life to be simple again. I just want to be a woman who's sneaking around on the guy she lives with."

I meant that as a sort of joke, an attempt to close the conversation by lightening the atmosphere, but it didn't work. Alison frowned and looked off into space, distressed. She sighed deeply and said, "Oh God, Chris. Please. Really. I don't know what Orin is up to, but I certainly don't have any hidden agenda. I thought I was being helpful, I really did."

Faintly, from the kitchen, I could hear talk, laughter, dishes rattling. I wished the attentive Frank would fill our water glasses: my head was pounding, my throat was tight and painful. I wondered if I had aspirin in my bag and, if I did, could I get it down. "And sometimes, what I really *really* want is for him to be Pierce. To be my old friend, back from the dead."

"Frankly, I think you're going to have to find out one way or another," she said. "That's the only way to end this madness. You're going to have to make some phone calls, do some checking."

"I wish you wouldn't *badger* me." I snapped this out; the kitchen noises suddenly ceased. Then, in the silence, we both laughed, surprising ourselves. She apologized again, and I felt suddenly warmer toward her—maybe only because she made me laugh. But I had a feeling we weren't going to be such friends after all.

My head ached. I wanted to leave—walk over to the Whitney, get some fresh air, look at the folk art, and then meet Orin and talk about something neutral, like whether the idea of putting a trolley line on 42nd Street was really feasible.

I tried to think of a way to leave gracefully, but Alison did it for me. She looked at her watch and said, with regret, "Oh hell, I should get going. I have this boring appointment in about ten minutes." She was the yuppie big-shot again, the woman with the bulging Filo-Fax.

She paid the check, insisted it could go on her expense account. Frank brought us our coats and helped us into them, out of the proper deferential politeness or a desire to get rid of us faster, I couldn't tell. On the sidewalk, Alison and I embraced. She kept hold of my arm and looked me in the eye. She said, "Chris. Forgive me. I know I've been nosy and intrusive and awful."

"No you haven't," I told her. "This talk has been good for me. It's helped me clarify things. I'm glad we got together, really I am." What I said was mostly true.

She shook her head. "No. I've upset you, I can see that. I'm a pain in the ass. And this whole thing is undoubtedly a dead end. I still think you should check it out, but Orin is probably just weird, and I'm trying to explain him with Pierce. I don't know what it is, maybe the business I'm in, working with these supremely rational *machines* all day, but I love the irrational, I love coincidence and mystery and fog and murk." She laughed and began to search in her purse for something, talking without looking at me. "The truth is, I had a real crush on Orin for a while, before I got hung up on Roger." She smiled to herself, down into the depths of her wine-colored bag. "He's such an odd duck—Orin. The mystery man. But he's really a very dear soul. I'm still extremely fond of him."

I couldn't help wondering if this was what she had wanted to tell me all along: this last, off-hand remark. *I had a real crush on Orin, I'm still extremely fond of him.* Was it Alison I should be wary of, after all? Alison's bright lipstick, painted fingernails, golden hair, way with waiters? I thought of Alison and Orin in his office at Parker Properties, putting their heads together over file servers and LAN networks. *I believe in pleasure.* The question was, what gave her pleasure?

She came up with what she was seeking: her business card—I remembered it from the train. She scribbled a phone number on the back and gave it to me, closing my hand around it. "Call me one of these days," she said. "Soon. We should talk some more—maybe when we've had less wine?" Her smile, I realized, was a little wobbly; she had drunk much more wine than I. "I mean it. I can be your sounding board. Lay any theory on me, no matter how absurd. And maybe we can go to an auction or something together. Okay? Will you call me?"

I set off toward Madison Avenue. The air felt wonderful—even in the middle of New York City, it was a lovely, fresh, May afternoon. I breathed deeply and felt myself waking up; my headache was immediately better. Alison and I were going in opposite directions, but I was tempted to look around, to see if she had really left or if she was still standing in front of Chez Duroc watching me with her glassy green eyes.

Chapter Ten

James showed me a postcard from my old friend Beth, in Taos. It arrived while I was in New York. In red ink, in her spiky handwriting it said: "So what's happening with you? Would it kill you to get in touch once in a while? Are you working? Are you painting? Are you still there? Hello? Love, Beth."

I read it and gave it back to him. James stood there holding it in his hand, looking at the color photograph of a black pottery bowl from San Ildefonso. "Nice bowl," he said.

"James." I didn't know how to go on.

"Before you think up another lie," he said, "let me also tell you that some guy called a couple of nights ago. It had that long-distance sound to it. He asked for Mary. I told him he had the wrong number."

"It could have been anybody," I said. I couldn't believe Orin would call me, get James, and not tell me about it.

"He's done it at least three times, maybe four. Same voice, same Mary." James held out the postcard with finger and thumb and let it drop to the polished floor at our feet. The black bowl gleamed up at us. "I know you're seeing someone in New York," James said. "Even without the postcard, even without the phone calls, I know what's been going on. You don't exactly have to be a genius to figure it out."

I broke down and told him about Orin. I told him everything, beginning with Alison on the train and ending with Beth's postcard. He knew about Pierce, of course—not everything, just that Pierce

was my friend, I loved him, he died young, and I had trouble accepting it. James had always been properly sympathetic. We always discussed Pierce's death along with our other losses, the various sorrows
from the difficult lives we lived before we met each other and became
happy together.

Now he didn't want to hear it. He said, "I don't give a damn about
the circumstances—all that this crap about Pierce means to me is that
you've been having an affair with some guy in New York and lying to
me about it."

He said he thought we should split up. He had been considering
selling the business. Raymond was trying to find a way to buy it, although this was a long shot no matter how good a deal James could
give him. But they were looking into it. James was ready for something else, he didn't know what. He'd been thinking of getting out of
New Haven. If we split up, he said, I could have the house and the
furniture and the cats.

Our talks went on all day and into the night. James didn't go to
work and we forgot to feed Rosy and Ruby. We didn't even answer
the phone. I imagined Orin, puzzled, on the other end; this didn't
bother me, it barely came through to me. What James told me was
devastating: all those months that I'd been deceiving him, he'd been
responding. I had thought he was merely sulky, and he had been out-
raged: he had been planning to leave me, to sell his business, to take
off for God knows where and leave our little house behind—leave me
behind because I had done him wrong. He had stopped being my savior, and who could blame him?

All this time, I had had no idea. I had joked about the situation
with Alison. I hadn't protested nearly enough when Orin made fun
of James.

Everything he said to me was brutal, and he made no attempt to
soften it. I was being punished. I was the fish hitting the cold water,
leaping in pain. His face was cold, closed, a stranger's face. The cats
wanted to get on his lap and he pushed them down. He didn't even
see them.

"You don't think I'm real," James said to me. "You don't think I'm
a real person, Chris."

"I do, James. That's not true."

He wouldn't listen to me. His fury was astonishing. He banged his fist down on table tops, he slammed doors, he couldn't eat, when the phone rang he turned on me and said, "Don't answer that!" He drank a can of beer and then squashed the can in his fist and tossed it at the wall. Beside this vehemence, I felt half-alive. I had no energy to shout back or to defend myself. I felt myself dwindling to nothing.

He asked me, "What in hell did you think was going through my mind all this time? Did you think I didn't notice? Did you think I didn't care? Did you think I'd just wait it out?"

"I haven't been thinking about anything." I didn't say that everything he said was true, though it was true: from the day Alison sat next to me on the train, James ceased to exist. What I said was, "I've been under an enchantment. I've been living in a dream."

He was not impressed, his anger intensified. He said, "This makes me wonder if that asshole Emile maybe didn't have a point when he sent you to the funny farm."

After that, we stopped discussing it. James slept in the guest room. I remained in our big brass bed, but I didn't sleep at all. As if to make up for all the months of neglect, I thought compulsively about James: how unhappy he was when we met, how it hurt him that he would never have a child of his own, how funny and sweet he was the day he delivered the cats to my apartment. I couldn't match his anger with any of my own. His accusations, the cruel things he said to me, even that final crack about the funny farm—none of them sparked anger, only a listless, defeated feeling, a sense that I'd been stupid, I'd been stupid again.

Lying there, with the cats draped over my legs—I tried to get one of them to go to James in the guest room, but they slept on our bed out of habit—I also thought about Denis, who would be in New Haven in less than three months. He was planning to spend a week with me and James before he had to report to Yale. I didn't want James to be gone when Denis came: the idea filled me with terror, and I realized what I had never understood before, that I was scared to death of my own son. I had been depending on James to make things pleasant between us, to help me smooth over the fact that, say what you might, I had let Emile take Denis away from me. I didn't fight, didn't get a lawyer, didn't even protest: I only sat quietly in my chair by the window in the funny farm, I waited until after visiting hours to cry. The two of them left for Paris, and I threw myself into the weaving of baskets. After a while I didn't cry anymore. Denis and I began writing our cordial little letters. My life went on.

I didn't know if Denis saw it that way or if he saw me as Emile's victim. I had no idea what Emile had told him. Denis and I had never discussed it. His letters were never anything but affectionate. But he was eighteen, and in person he might want a confrontation: this might, indeed, be the real reason he was coming to Yale. He terrified me, and now James expected me to face him alone.

I lay on the bed we had shared, thinking about Denis—the sweetness of his childhood. I was filled with terror. I knew that James was lying awake across the hall, and I was unable to go to him. I was unable to beg him to stay. I didn't know if I wanted him to, and if I had known that I wanted him to, I still couldn't have asked him.

Orin was not on my mind at all, but all that week I knew I'd go to New York on Saturday as usual. James asked me nothing, and I didn't tell him that I was going: it was assumed. I called a taxi while he was at work. When the taxi pulled up in front and honked, and I picked up my overnight bag and went out the front door and locked it behind me, it felt final, as if it were the last time. I imagined coming home to find James gone, and I almost told the taxi driver to forget it, I almost went back inside and called James at Jimmy Luigi's, broke down weeping and asked him to forgive me. I was pretty sure that he would, and so I didn't do it.

~

I asked Orin why he didn't tell me about James answering the phone when he called. "I thought it would just confuse the issue," he said. It was the same answer he gave me when I asked him why he never told me he'd been an actor.

What issue? This is what I wanted to ask him, but I didn't see the point.

He wanted to know about the lunch with Alison. "What did you talk about?"

"Antique furniture."

He laughed. "You didn't talk about men?"

"William Morris," I told him. "Gustav Stickley."

After my lunch with Alison Orin seemed different to me. I trusted him less—or I admitted to myself that I had never really trusted him, I wasn't sure which. Many of the things he said seemed insincere, or deliberately superficial. He looked more like Pierce. He was in a good mood, full of beans but I didn't want to talk to him, I just wanted to be in bed with him, making love and sleeping and making love again. I kept wondering if Proust ever considered the possibility that a random memory found in a cup of tea could be the kind of memory that did no one any good, or that *temps perdu* ought to stay lost.

I didn't tell Orin about James's discovery. I said only that I was thinking of breaking up with James, that living with him had become painful. Orin smiled slightly when I said this, as he did whenever I mentioned James. We had just come back from dinner, and we were sitting side by side on the sofa in the living room. Orin said, "So what would you do? Move into the city? Get a job? Or can you support yourself painting?"

"I'm not sure. James said he'd let me have the house."

Orin laughed. "Thanks a lot, buddy. Your payments are pretty enormous, right?"

"Pretty enormous, yeah."

"I'll tell you what," he said. "Sell the place and move into New York. I'll find you something you can afford, and I'll figure out a way for you to finance it." At first I thought he was kidding—his sleazy realtor routine—but he sat up straight and faced me, and I could see the enthusiasm in his face. "This is the time to buy," he said. "With interest rates going down, things are really going to start to move. You've got to do it now, Chris."

I sat there half-listening, watching him. He had been leafing through the newspaper, and he had his spectacles on. He was wearing a denim shirt and a black knitted tie. He looked very sharp, very handsome. The shirt made his eyes look intensely blue. Was I imagining it that Pierce once wore a black tie and a denim shirt like this when he worked in a bank?

"I'll help you find a job, too," Orin said. "In fact, a friend of mine in the business happens to need a receptionist. Steve Kramer—a really nice guy, and he pays well, and basically all you're doing is answering the phone and making appointments. Then we could forget this weekend stuff, we'd get a lot more time together, Chris." He held my hand, squeezing my fingers together, full of his fantasies. "I just want to be with you," he said. "You've changed my life. You wouldn't believe how lonely I used to be, how lonely this city can be." He pulled me roughly over to him, my head against his blue shirt. He said into my hair, "Ah, you know I love you, Chrissie. I'm sick of putting you on that damned 2:00 train and sending you back to the pizza capital of New England." He laughed. "Come on, admit it—wouldn't it be great if you lived here?"

Yes, it would be great. I said it to him, I said it to myself: I can sell the Bishop Street house and move into a condominium in Manhattan and work in a real estate office and see Orin all the time. I felt an unfocused disappointment. What did I expect him to say? I had the same feeling I used to have when I put on my white mini-dress and stockings and took the bus to Dr. Mankoff's office after a weekend of painting. The idea went through my head: *he's not who I thought he was.* This seemed absurd to me: of course he wasn't, that was the whole point.

The next morning, when he was in the shower, I searched his apartment again. I didn't know what I was looking for now, it just seemed important to me to know who he was, to find out something I didn't know—anything. I had uncovered all his dirty socks, his underwear, his collection of shirt cardboard. I had looked at all this books and shaken them to see what fell out, I had gone through his pockets, I had stood on a chair to inspect the back of the closet shelf, opened his suitcase, looked at the labels in his sweaters, gone through the kitchen cupboards. I looked now in more deliberate hiding places: under the pile of sheets in the linen closet, in the toes of the shoes on his closet floor, under the sofa cushions. I looked for hidden drawers and fake bottoms. I considered opening the packages of frozen spinach to see if they contained spinach or a collection of letters from me to Pierce tied up in ribbon. I stopped short of that; nor did I take down the posters on the wall to look for a hidden safe, or pour out the All-Bran to see what was in the bottom of the box.

But I did lift the mattress and find a gun.

Orin was whistling in the shower, as he often did. He was whistling "Cheek to Cheek." He was a very good whistler. It struck me for the first time that if you can whistle in tune you can sing in tune.

The gun looked to me like Pierce's .38. Maybe it didn't, maybe it was just that all guns would look alike to me. But it seemed to me that I would know it anywhere, the shape, the grey sheen. The aura of evil was the same, the ominous look of it. I didn't even know if it was loaded, but just holding it gingerly in my hand, I imagined something horrible happening, as if by its very existence the gun could do harm. I could see Pierce's hand, I could see him give the gun to Robbie, Robbie pointing it at a gull, putting it to his temple. *Ka-boom*. I was sitting on the floor beside Pierce's bed. I had a mad impulse to point the gun and shoot it—point at anything, just to pull the trigger. To get it over with.

This impulse was so strong that I had to set the gun down. It was a moment of horror, of such giddiness that I thought I was going to be sick. I leaned against the side of the bed and closed my eyes, and the moment passed. Orin was still whistling. Sunlight streamed in the window. I was wearing underpants and the denim shirt Orin had had on last night. The bed was unmade, the yellow sheets rumpled. A few minutes ago Orin and I had been lying in it, pleasing each other in all the ways we'd learned to do these past months. Before long, we would go out for brunch. There was a little place we always went that made good Bloody Marys and a jalapeño quiche we both liked.

I looked at the gun. It couldn't be the same one. Obviously. The police confiscated that gun after Robbie shot himself. They traced it to Pierce, who had been dead for three months, and concluded quite logically that Robbie got it from Pierce. This was a different gun.

The shower stopped, and I shoved the gun back where I had found it. It couldn't be the same one. And yet it was. Like Orin and Pierce: different and yet the same.

~

The following Monday, I called information and got the number for St. Paul's School. I told the woman who answered the phone that I needed to get in touch with an alumnus and she connected me with Records. I told the woman in Records that I was planning a surprise for my husband, I was trying to get together his old friends from school: did they have some kind of alumni directory, did she by any chance have an update on Orin Pierce, class of 1960? I spelled it for her. She was gone for quite a while. When she came back she said she'd checked '59 and '61 as well, and she really couldn't understand it, there was no Orin Pierce listed at all. There was nobody at St. Paul's by that name. Was there some mistake?

Maybe, I said. Maybe I had got the year wrong, I would double-check. And what about Mr. Thompson, the music teacher? Was he still around?

~

I asked James, "What if I just quit seeing him?"

James didn't know. He had to think about it. Maybe we could try to work things out, but it wouldn't be easy. What he didn't get is why I started seeing this guy in the first place.

"I mean, forget the Pierce stuff," he said. "What about me? You weren't just having some fantasy about getting your old pal Pierce back. You were rejecting me, Chris. Why was that? How could you do that to me? What's the matter between us?"

We went over it and over it. When I explained, it sounded stupid. I remembered when I had told Charlie on the phone last winter, how convincing it seemed. James said sorry, it didn't make any sense. He could understand wanting to track down this guy because he might be Pierce—or not *understand* it but sympathize with it, he could see that this might be something I could get hung up on. Beyond that, he didn't get it. Why hadn't I told him about it? Why had I ended up in bed with this guy?

I had no answers to these questions. I couldn't remember my thought processes. I kept telling him I hadn't had any thought pro-cesses. I hadn't been thinking at all, I'd been reacting, I'd been living in a dream.

"So why is it over?" he wanted to know. "Why are you willing to quit seeing him? Why do you want me to stay with you? Why don't you just go live with this real estate bozo if he's so fucking wonderful? Jesus!" He slammed his fist down on the table, he dropped his head into his hands and pulled at his hair until it stood up in clumps. His hair was getting very grey, and I noticed that the pigtail was gone, he'd cut it off. "Mr. Cool," he said. "Mr. Sleazeball. Tell me what you see in this guy."

I didn't tell him how much he sounded like Orin. I kept saying, "I don't know, James." I couldn't think of anything else to say. I couldn't say: *Stay with me, I'm afraid*—the words I couldn't say to Emile— maybe I should have, and maybe I should have said them now. Or I should have told James that Orin was my pigtail, my last gasp before middle age set in. Maybe it really was that simple, that I took a lover because I didn't want to get old. How delightfully commonplace it sounded. How *mainstream,* as Silvie might say.

He said, "I don't know if we should stay together or not. I don't know who you are anymore, and I don't know if I ever knew who I was."

We went over it and over it until we were both too tired to talk anymore. We were falling asleep at the kitchen table. I wanted him to sleep with me in our bed, but he wouldn't, said he couldn't. He said I was breaking his heart. We clung to each other in the upstairs hall and then he went off to the guest room.

Stay with me, I'm afraid. The cats settled on my legs. Dawn came in stripes through the window shutters.

Orin called me the next afternoon. James was at work. It was Orin's regular day to call, but I forgot that until the phone rang. I an- swered the phone in the bedroom, and as soon as I heard Orin's voice I saw the gun. I felt its evil grey shape in my hand, the cold warmth of it.

Orin said, "I'm having a rotten week, one frustration after another, and I've got to go out for drinks with that Chapman guy I told you about. The guy who wants to unload all those rent-controlled build- ings? God. Deliver me. And I've missed you like crazy. I wish to hell you'd do what we were talking about. Move to the city. I wish you were here right this minute. I need you, Chris. This place is a jungle, it's no joke."

He sounded perfectly normal. He couldn't know I had seen the gun. I said to him, "I called St. Paul's."

"You what?" He was laughing, his voice full of affection. "Ah Chrissie," he said. "Chrissie, you're too much, you're wonderful. So you finally did it. And what did St. Paul's say?"

"You know what St. Paul's said."

"I guess the bribe wasn't big enough," Orin said, and chuckled.

"Why do you tell me these lies?"

"Hey," he said. "Honey. Is this such a big deal? You know how many guys there are in this world who lie about what prep school they go to? What college? I really did go to Columbia, though. I've got a diploma to prove it, down at my mother's somewhere. But I confess: I didn't go to St. Paul's. I went to Sarasota High. I would have given anything to go to prep school up in New England, but— you know."

"But what?"

"We weren't exactly rolling in it," he said. "My father was a carpenter—sort of a carpenter, mostly he did odd jobs. My mother worked for a while in a curtain shop. I had to work my way through Columbia. It took me six years. Listen," he said. "When I see you this weekend, I'll tell you all about my unpleasant childhood. Is that what you want? Chrissie? Listen. Any little lie I've told you was just to make you love me. Do you understand? I'm serious about this. Do you understand?"

No one ever loved me the way you loved Pierce.

Me either, Orin.

"Yes," I told him. "I do understand."

"This weekend I'll spill it all," he said. "Promise. Whatever you want to know. Okay? I'll even call Mom, you can talk to her. I'll call her and tell her I've met the woman of my dreams."

I wanted to ask him about the gun, but I didn't.

Why do you have a gun, Orin?

For protection in the big city. I told you Chrissie—it's a jungle. The city is full of bad guys, me among them.

I saw the dark sea-blue of his eyes, I heard his laugh.

❧ Chapter Eleven

I began a letter to Charlie: *Help me, I don't know what I'm doing, a lot has happened since I talked to you, I met the man I told you about and he's not who I thought he was, I don't know who he is.* I ripped this up and started over: *Can you still not accept it that he's dead? I can't accept it, I'm not accepting it any better than I ever did, what can I do, Charlie, I've gotten into a mess, help me.* I ripped it up. I ripped them all up. They were nothing but hysterics, and that was not what I wanted, that was not what I meant. I couldn't seem to get anything straight. I kept trying to explain, to understand, but the conversations I had with Charlie in my head were rambling and incoherent. I dialed his number out in California and hung up on the first ring because I couldn't think what to say.

Denis was writing to me often. He was excited. He'd read *Bright Lights, Big City.* He had a new Nirvana album. He had bought some new American clothes. Polo shirts, red suspenders, a pair of Ralph Lauren jeans: should he start wearing the jeans now or wait until he got to New Haven? Would it be better to bring them slightly worn or brand new? I left his letters unanswered; when I saw the blue envelopes in the mailbox, I was terrified, as if they were something alive that could harm me.

I was supposed to call Alison, but I didn't. Hugh and Helga came back from their honeymoon and invited us to dinner, but we put them off. I didn't plant pansies along our front walk, I didn't go outside and deadhead the tulips in the back yard, I didn't divide the iris or prune the black tips off the rosebushes. I should have called Silvie, to gloat about Denis getting into Yale without my interference, but I didn't do that either. I should have written to assure Beth that I was indeed alive, except that I wasn't sure that it was true.

I hadn't been painting since James found out about Orin. I was finding it impossible to paint—partly because it seemed so much trouble. I was sluggish, I had no ambition. It was hard enough to get out of bed every day—much less set up my paints and the blue Mason jars full of water. The landscapes and the portrait-montages that had absorbed me all winter and spring looked merely strange to me, the work of someone I had met, was not very well acquainted with, and had no desire to know better. I had been asked to participate in a group show in the fall with three other local painters at a New Haven Gallery, and I accepted, but the fall which seemed imminent when I thought of Denis seemed otherwise impossibly far away. The future was another country, as lost and remote as Tibet.

I began drawing, working with a fine black felt-tip pen. I drew anything—plain, large, bleak representations of my feet, the clothes hanging in my closet, the dishes in the sink. Everything looked good to me done in this medium. The thin definiteness of the line transformed the world as I had begun to see it: it gave the world some coherence that I found not consoling perhaps but agreeable.

I couldn't decide if I was unhappy or not—I knew I should be unhappy, but when inspected my state of mind I could detect only various kinds of panic.

I hardly ever saw James. He worked long hours at Jimmy Luigi's, and in the evenings he began going to movies by himself. The movies distracted him. He didn't know what he wanted to do. He couldn't even think about it anymore. He wanted time to pass, he wanted to see what would happen. He couldn't be around me, he said; his jealousy was like a physical pain. Just being in the same room with me tortured him. Even if I should quit seeing Orin, even if Orin no longer meant anything to me, he didn't know if that would change anything. When he looked at me, all he could remember was that we were once happy together, and his happy memories made the pain worse.

This reminded me of a passage I used to like in Proust, something about Swann's jealousy of Odette, but I couldn't quite place it, and I didn't have the will to look it up.

I had a feeling that James was waiting for me to act, but I didn't know what action to take. *I'll stop seeing Orin,* I told him, but he didn't ask *when,* and he didn't give me any guarantees, and he wouldn't talk about it. I would have liked to tell him the whole truth about Orin—about St. Paul's, about the gun, about his changes from Orin to Pierce and back again in the blink of an eye, the way leaves change from light to dark in the wind—but James didn't want to hear it. I tried to tell him my fears about Denis, and he said he couldn't cope with that now. I wanted to say: *Don't leave me, I'm afraid,* but our house was full of silences that I didn't have the energy to break.

James would pick up catfood at the store, bring it home, put it away in the cupboard, and go out to a late movie, not saying a word.

～

Cher Denis,

I think it's wonderful that you'll be coming to Yale. I don't think I've congratulated you properly on getting in. Good work, my dearest! There are plenty of New Haveners who dislike the university and resent all those Yalies clogging the narrow old streets and swelling the lines at the movie theaters and restaurants, but I always feel good when I see them: they so often look like nice people, the kind of interesting, fearless, lively people I liked when I was that age. I can't help but think that you're going to be very happy there. I look forward to your coming. I haven't seen you in so long. I can't wait to see what you look like in your red suspenders! And Denis, I hope you don't bear me any ill will for seeing you so seldom all these years—for not traveling to France myself, and not sending you the airfare to come here in the summers. You do understand, I hope, that my financial situation has always been precarious, but not only that—I've always felt, too, that Emile would discourage much visiting between us, and I'm afraid I've gone along with that, out of timidity—out of downright fear. I can see now that I should have never let you go in the first place, back when Emile and I were divorced. But it was a hard time for me, I don't know what he's told you, probably plenty of lies and distortions mixed with the truth, but when your father left me I was not myself, and he took advantage of my weakness, he—

I ripped this letter up, too.

～

The next time I saw Orin, he said, "So Chrissie. Come on. Ask me. Let's play Twenty Questions." But I couldn't think of any questions. I had, at some deep level, ceased to want answers from him.

Orin talked to Steve Kramer, who was very interested in interviewing me for the job. Orin wanted to set up an appointment. He also said I should be getting the house on the market. Time's a-wasting, he said.

"Orin, James and I haven't even got this all figured out yet," I told him. "I haven't decided what I want to do about the house."

"You mean James hasn't decided," Orin said. He kept asking me, "Why don't you be the one who makes the decision? Why don't you kick him out instead of waiting for him to tell you he's going? That way you get the psychological advantage. Let's face it, Chris, you're going to split up eventually, you know that. Why not now, so you can get going with your life?"

Talking was becoming difficult, we argued so much. We spent a lot of time in museums. This was not at all as I used to tell James: I wasn't inspired by what I saw, I was depressed—overwhelmed by the intensity of the paintings we looked at. At the Museum of Modern Art, in front of Van Gogh's "Starry Night," I was struck by how menacing the sky looked—all those blue whirling stars like bombs— and how vulnerable the town below. I knew from reading his letters that Van Gogh was not cruel, he was a gentle soul, and yet the painting struck me as cruel. I was reminded of my old quarrel with "The Night Café," how I couldn't see any passion in it. Orin said, "It's so unjust that this poor bastard's paintings are now selling for millions," and standing there with my arm through his, I began to cry.

On a hot Sunday in the middle of June, Orin and I went out as usual for brunch. The streets had never seemed so dismal before— the heat baking up from the pavements, the bodies of drunks propped up in their own urine, whole armies of the homeless on street corners with their grocery carts full of rags, their hollow-eyed children, their outstretched hands. Orin always emptied a couple of rolls of quarters into his jacket pocket on Sundays and handed them out until they were gone. This always startled me. He never said a word about it, or about the people who reached out their hands, and he never spoke to these people—merely nodded if they said thank you, ignored them if they didn't.

After brunch, we walked back to his place to pick up my bag. We were late, hurrying in the heat. Orin was irritable. He said, "Why don't you just forget it? Go back later when it's cool? Why do you have to get this particular train?"

"Because I always do."

"Mr. Pizza isn't even there—right? He won't know what time you get in. And what difference does it make, anyway, if you're splitting up?"

We bickered about this point all the way to 57th Street. We often argued about this on Sunday afternoons—our old quarrel: what time I was going back to New Haven, *why* I was going back to New Haven. Orin was impatient with me. I'd been cold and withdrawn, he said, or else I snapped at him. And I was refusing to deal with the James situation. And refusing to deal with the Pierce situation. And there were things I wasn't telling him, like why I broke down at the museum. Also, the air-conditioning in his apartment had been erratic. There were nights when we just lay there side by side, too hot and too irritable to make love.

On the elevator going upstairs, Orin said, "In my opinion, you haven't broken up with James yet because you're afraid to commit yourself to me."

I didn't have an answer for this; it seemed both obvious and beside the point.

"Am I right?" Orin asked. "Is that accurate, would you say?"

I told him I didn't know. He took my wrist and held it tightly in his right hand. His hand was tanned a warm brown, my arm was so white it looked bleached. He held my wrist until we got to his door, and then he let it go. Where he'd held it, there was a mottled bracelet of red on the dead-white skin.

I folded my nightgown and put it in my bag. I found a pair of earrings on the night table and tucked them away in my purse. Orin fussed awhile with the air conditioner, which was not working, then went into the bathroom. After I straightened out the bedclothes, I sat down for a moment on the edge of the bed and stared out the window. Opposite, there was a yellow brick building, a row of windows covered by tan drapes.

There was something wrong with the day—this sunny Sunday morning in New York. I kept thinking about what happened to me at the Museum of Modern Art. Orin was angry because I couldn't explain what was so upsetting; all I could say was no, it's not the millions, it's not the irony of it, it's not the Bloody Marys I had at brunch. I still couldn't explain it, but I couldn't get the innocent town and the exploding stars out of my mind.

I heard Orin pee into the toilet, then I heard water running. I was imagining what it would be like to live in that quiet town, unaware of the wild stars, the violence over my head—how terrible that would be: better to know. I stood up, holding my breath, and reached under the mattress. The gun was still there. I shoved it into my overnight bag and zipped it up. The toilet flushed. Orin came out of the bathroom and we walked to the train.

~

James was going to California—not right away, probably in a couple of weeks. And not to stay, just as a sort of trial. He knew a couple of people out there—he mentioned the Rosenthals, whom I'd met, and somebody named Greg, whom I hadn't. He wouldn't sell the business just yet. Raymond could run it while he was gone—for two or three months, he couldn't say for sure. He and Raymond would see how things went. Meanwhile, James might try to get into the restaurant business out on the coast. Or he might just buy himself a houseboat and drift for a while. The important thing was that he get away.

Get away from you, is what he meant. I was reminded of Emile, who escaped to France. But James was very courteous, very considerate—almost the old James. He no longer reproached me. Evenings, we sat together with the cats, watching television in the living room, me on the pressback oak rocker, James on the Victorian love seat we had shopped for together the summer before. I tried to keep my attention on the television programs, but they meant nothing to me, and when they were over I couldn't have said what all the laughing was about or who the characters were. James and I talked a little during commercials—mostly James. He said we could do it gradually, meaning split up. He meant it when he said the house was mine. It wasn't much of a gift, he said—there was a huge mortgage, and I might want to consider selling it; in fact, the market was looking good, he had made a few inquiries on my behalf.

He was over his hard feelings. He hoped we wouldn't become enemies over this. He would always care for me, always hope I was doing well. He was looking ahead, and he hoped I was too. He was sure he'd be getting the word one of these days that I was having a big show in New York. "A retrospective," he said. "Or are you too young for a retrospective?" He made his little jokes. His brown eyes, when I dared to look at them, seemed inexpressibly sad.

"I hoped we could work this out," I said to him once.

"Well, you're usually right about things, Chris," he said. "But this time I don't think so."

～

I dream about Emile. I am trying to paint a still life, a vase of yellow flowers. Emile is standing beside my easel. He is very tall, even taller probably than he really is, just as the dream flowers are yellower and more vibrant than any flowers in the real world.

Emile is scolding me. Hurry, he keeps saying. You've got to go faster. Come on, damn it. Hurry.

I am finding it hard to paint any faster. I want to paint beautifully. I am trying to put in every detail. I want my painting to be as perfect as life is, as complete. Hurry up, Emile says. He looms over me, he casts a shadow. His presence slows me down. If he would just shut up and go away, I could work faster, I could finish my painting. Come on, come on.

Then I see why he is so desperate: as I look, as I move my brush across the paper, dip it in water, pick up paint, wipe the brush, approach the paper again—as I do this over and over, mixing colors, making every brush stroke perfect, as I do this, I can see that the flowers are drooping. They are dying. Even as I watch, even as I move as fast as I can from water to palette to paper, the flowers are drooping, they're drying up, they're fading, they're dropping their petals, they're dead.

~

It had taken me a long time—years, forever, half my life—but I saw at last that I had to do something, and I knew what it was. I left the next day as soon as James went to work—late morning. I fed Ruby and Rosie, then drove out Whitney Avenue to my favorite gas station, the Sunoco place where they still pumped the gas for you, and checked the oil and washed the windshield. I stopped at a deli and picked up a can of rootbeer and a cheese sandwich so I wouldn't have to stop for lunch. My overnight bag was on the floor beside me: underwear, shorts, sweatshirt, toothbrush, gun. As I drove over the river and picked up I-95, it occurred to me that the date was close to the anniversary of the night Charlie came up my back stairs to tell me Pierce was dead, twenty-one years ago.

As I drove, it was as if a spell had been lifted, or a door long closed had been thrown open: I was able to think about Pierce the way I used to before I ran into Alison on the train. The old Pierce—not the Pierce who kept changing, the Pierce I couldn't get into focus, but the true Pierce, the Pierce I loved, returned to me.

I remembered the morning he came into the dining hall in his old green army cap, watched me eating oatmeal, and said, "Do you really like that stuff, or do you just eat it to be weird?"

I remembered when he came back from Cleveland with a Bessie Smith record, how we sat in his room holding hands, not talking, just listening to "Empty Bed Blues" and "Long Old Road."

I remembered when he read Van Gogh's letters and got so hung up on Van Gogh—how angry he was at the injustices of Van Gogh's sad, saintly life.

I remembered when his hair got long and curled around his shoulders and he wore a leather headband we bought at a peace demonstration on the New Haven Green.

I remembered the summer he visited us in Jamesville, how he charmed my mother because he was so funny, and pleased my father because he worked hard for no pay, and skipped flat stones across the pond with Robbie and me, imitating the mating calls of frogs.

I remembered him as Horatio, with Hamlet dead in his arms, saying *Good night, sweet prince* into a hushed silence.

~

Just north of Boston, I ate my cheese sandwich, but before long I was hungry again, and warm, so I got off the highway at Ogunquit and bought an ice cream cone, which I ate sitting on a bench looking down over the ocean. The waves leapt up the rocks, dashing spray into the air, and subsided back into the dark blue ocean that was the color of Pierce's eyes. The water was like a restless animal.

I took a walk down the main street, where the sun and the blue sky made everything shine. The extreme and unseasonable heat had abated, we had had rain, and the leaves of the trees were dark and glossy. The street was lined with seafood places, craft shops with decoys in the windows, deli-type markets where you could buy cheese and chocolate and fruit-flavored teas. The souvenir shops I remembered from the trip with Pierce and Robbie were gone; maybe they were disguised as boutiques. I couldn't find the diner where we pumped black coffee into Pierce, but it didn't matter. The town was crowded and friendly, it smelled of sand and fish and seaweed, and the sky over the horizon was cerulean blue. The town reminded me of James. I thought of him with pleasure, even with hope: James with the heart of gold, James who waltzed with me on the ice, and who talked to the cats as if they were his children.

The panic that gripped me in New Haven and New York, that dogged everything I did, had faded mysteriously away. This was what I had been needing, then: these familiar blues and greens, the huge sky, the sea struggling against the rocks.

～

I stayed overnight in a motel in Camden—not the one where my mother and I giggled over the Magic Fingers. This motel was more like the one my parents used to run—a family place, with cabins. The woman in the office wore an apron and t-shirt; she looked as if she had been interrupted in the middle of making bread. She gave me a schedule for the ferry, as well as a coupon for a dollar off a lobster dinner at the same restaurant where my mother and I ate. My key was attached by a chain to a plastic seashell. My mother would have appreciated the cabin: it was spotless, white-painted inside and out, with a lumpy mattress on an iron bedstead, a chenille spread, and a bunch of daisies on the nightstand. There was a television, but I didn't turn it on. I fell asleep early, my overnight bag with the gun in it tucked down at the end of the bed by my feet.

The ferry was scheduled to leave at eight, and I was at the dock by 7:30 to buy my ticket. Sometimes it got crowded, the motel woman had told me: first come, first served. I was in plenty of time. "Good day for it," the ticket seller said. For what? For anything. The sun shone on the water in a shower of golden coins.

Once we were at sea, the ocean breeze was cool, and I put on the sweatshirt I'd remembered to bring. Halfway there, I realized I should also have brought some supplies—a scrubbing brush, rags, Mr. Clean. I should have brought food and drink. I could think only of the gun, which was in the bottom of my purse wrapped tightly in a plastic bag. I hadn't even brought my sketch pad. There was no store on the island—at least, there didn't used to be, and when I asked a woman sitting near me on the deck, she said, "Mercy no," as if the islanders had no need of stores, as if their only legitimate needs were rocks and gulls.

"I hope you didn't forget anything," she said.

"Nothing important."

From the ferry, I could look back and see the church spire rising over the town, and the cluster of white houses along the road that hugged the curve of the harbor. The ferry was running regularly again; it seemed newer than the one my mother and I escaped on, but nothing else had changed much. Plover Island looked precisely the same: the wild shoreline dotted with seabirds, the far-flung cottages, and our old cabin at the end of the sandy road, weathered and tumble-down, perched on its rocky little hill like something thrown up by the sea.

Before I approached it, I took a walk around the island, skirting the rocky incline up to the cabin and heading down the level, dusty road that led away. There were wild roses along the road, blue morning glories climbing a wall, two kids on bicycles, a dog tied to a wooden clothespole. One cottage had undergone a posh remodel (Palladian window, skylights, latticework deck) but most of them were simple shingled structures with yards full of sand and beach-grass. I half-expected to run into the woman painter in her sun hat, or the two talkative old men with plums. Or Pierce and Robbie catching crabs down by the rocks. I wished, as I often had, that the miracle would occur and Robbie would come again to sit with me drinking tea from Gran's old pot. Or Pierce himself: if he appeared suddenly in the path before me wearing his denim shirt, his army cap—what a gift, what inexpressible solace.

How stingy the dead can be, I thought, but I felt no resentment at the thought.

The sun was climbing in the sky. The purse slung over my shoulder was cumbersome, heavier by the moment. I took off the sweatshirt and tied it around my waist. I imagined the interior of the cabin, dark and musty, with a slight chill. I went down by the rocks, took off my sneakers and cooled my feet in the water, and then, my heart beating fast, I climbed the hill to the cabin.

The lock was broken, but when I pushed open the door I didn't see what I had expected: no one had trashed it, burned it out, spraypainted dirty words on the walls. Everything looked the same—just worse. It had been thirteen years. The cabin hadn't gone unused: there was a pile of empty beer cans on the old bookcase, a plastic grocery bag hanging from a doorknob, a ticking pillow split open, a squashed cardboard carton that wasn't there before. But it looked long-abandoned, except by mice and spiders and dust and mold. The place smelled terrible, a combination of ocean and animals and musty air and rotting wood.

I didn't stay inside long. I inspected everything, gingerly. I realized that a scrub brush and pail wouldn't have gotten me very far. The cabin was reverting to what it always longed to be: a pile of rubble. It cared about the presence of humans as much as the sea did, the rocks. I had been half-wondering if it would be possible to rehabilitate it, to make it into a memorial not to Robbie dead but to Robbie alive: the brother who came up here to drink beer and catch fish and play poker, not the one who held a gun to his skull and pulled the trigger. I had been thinking of coming here summers with James, of fixing it up as we did the house: James and me in a sunny room filled with old white wicker furniture. But the cabin was beyond saving, and I didn't really mind. This way, it belonged to Robbie: it was always his, if it was anyone's at all. *Take it,* I said aloud, hoping I would get an answer, but the only sound besides my footsteps was the faint dash of the waves on the rocks down below.

I walked down to the beach and sat with my arms around my knees. The sun beat down on my head. I should have brought a hat, I should have brought a can of something to drink. The ferry would return at five: it seemed a long way off. I had hoped to stay until sunset, maybe even sleep on the beach all night, but this was not possible, I would have to go back.

I stretched out on the sand and fell into a light, uneasy doze. Fitfully, I dreamed about the cabin as it was when Emile and I cleaned it out. *Denis runs around, he is wearing blue shorts, a red-striped shirt, he is shouting questions and raising dust.* The dream came and went; I was conscious that it was a dream, and that the dream was half memory. *Denis is small, joyful, perfect: my son. And suddenly, he's gone—just disappeared. Impossible, but it has happened. We look everywhere but he can't be found. Emile says he must have been stolen by Tom, the man who ferried us out: remember how well they got along, he says, remember how much Denis liked him. It was Tom, Emile says. But I know it was Emile, and I fling myself on him, hitting him with my fists, and he crumples at my attack, there is blood, he cries out, he tries to shield himself with his hands, and though I know it's only a dream, though I feel the sand under my back and hear the water beat against the rocky shore, I hit him until he lies still.*

I opened my eyes to find that the sun had gone behind a cloud. The sea was grey and choppy, the sky a less intense blue, but it was still warm, and my face was hot and tight, probably sunburned. I didn't feel well—the horrible dream was still vividly with me. I sat up, took my hairbrush from my purse to brush my hair back from my face, and wiped my face with a tissue. I turned my mind from the dream, and from the consciousness of how thirsty I was. All around me there were fat gulls standing on the rocks. They paid no attention to me. I wondered if I was merging with the elements just as the cabin was. I looked out at the sea, and at the church steeple rising above the town. This was where we sat out on the rocks. This was where Pierce took out the gun and aimed it at the gulls.

Why do you have that gun?

For protection in the big bad city.

I thought about how it could have happened, how he didn't die, how he could have become a balding Manhattan businessman. He would have been doing drugs in New Mexico, hard stuff, Lord knows what—not pot or peyote or LSD but something Charlie and I had never even heard of, something nobody did anymore. Pierce would try anything. And he lent his car to someone, and when his car went off the cliff he was tripping, he was out of commission for days. And then he was confused, disoriented. At some point he would hear about his own death. He would get a kick out of that. And then he would worry about me, Charlie, his parents, his old girlfriends. He would want to return and reassure us, but—

I couldn't go any further. It was absurd. It was like one of those improbable movies from the fifties that featured amnesia and shrinking men and death rays that wiped out the entire populations of sleepy little New England towns. I put my head down on my knees. Pierce was dead. He'd been dead for twenty-one years, almost to the day.

I was so thirsty I was tempted to drink sea water. I thought of books I'd read about shipwrecked people, movies about people stuck in a lifeboat with a pint of water that had to last until they were rescued. The fifties were big on shipwreck movies, too—people always went out of their heads from thirst. I wondered if that was happening to me. I considered knocking on a door, and asking for a drink of water, but I didn't do it. I wasn't that far gone, I told myself. I was bored, hot, hungry, tired. The gulls didn't move. The rocks were their kingdom—the rocks and the sea, which was like cold wavy glass, bluish grey near the shore with a hint of green farther out. I tried to remember why I came to the island. It seemed to me that I had come to find Pierce and Robbie, but at one time I had something else in mind, though I couldn't recall what it was.

I walked up to the cabin. Maybe, miraculously, someone had left a can of intact beer or a bottle of water. The door swung on its hinges. The hinges were rusty—hopeless. Inside, I looked in the middle of the front room and watched the dust. The air was vibrating slightly, the dust was never still—even in the dimness, with no sunlight to come in through the filthy windows, I could see the dust move. All around me, spiders hung motionless in their webs. Somewhere there were mice. Maybe there were other animals, but I couldn't hear them, I couldn't hear anything. From the cabin, even the sea was almost quiet.

I wondered who had been here, who left the beer cans and the pillow. There were no homeless people on Plover Island, no derelicts, no bag ladies. It was teenagers, probably, who came over from Camden to drink and fool around: how perfect, a deserted cabin. I imagined them groping each other on the filthy floor, bleary-eyed kids with their lives ahead of them. Not knowing what ghosts prowl here.

Robbie, I said out loud. *Pierce.*

I remembered when Pierce gave Robbie the gun. I remembered that I lay back against Pierce, his lips against my neck. He said, "Chrissie Chrissie Chrissie," and I stopped thinking about Robbie. I barely noticed what he was doing—aiming at gulls, aiming at rocks. And then he raised the gun to his temple. . . .

I'm sitting on the floor under the window. It has gotten darker. Have I missed the ferry? How long have I been here? I look at my watch. The ferry must have come and gone. I stand up, with effort. I'm stiff. Out the window, I see that the sun is a scarlet globe low over the town, and the sky is purple and rose. I stare into the sun, watching the golden path widen across the water. Soon the light will be gone, the stars will explode overhead.

Behind me, there's a noise. I turn, and he's there—just like that. How strange to see him here. He looks out of place in the doorway—and then I realize that I myself must look out of place here. The cabin is a work of nature, it's not meant for us.

"Chrissie," he says. "I came to get you. Come with me. Down to the rocks where we can talk."

He turns and goes out the door, and I follow him, walking down the rocky slope to the sand, following his back to the beach. It doesn't occur to me not to go. My bag bumps against my legs. He wears his denim shirt. We sit down on the warm sand, not touching; he smiles at me.

He says, "Why did you come up here all by yourself, Chrissie?"

"I can't remember," I tell him.

"It was a crazy thing to do."

"Probably."

"I've been missing you," he says, and his smile deepens. I would know his smile anywhere, the ironic curl to it, and the raised eyebrow. His eyes are exactly the color of the sea. I pull my bag closer to me and open it. Inside I can feel the gun, cold in its plastic.

"I've missed you, too," I say.

"It's me, you know," he says. He pays no attention to the gun. His eyes don't even flicker toward it. "It really is me, Chrissie. I can prove it, there are lots of ways."

"I don't need you to prove it. I know who you are."

"Ah," he says. "Good." He looks out to sea, away from the burning sun. Of course. His profile against the sky is exactly the same. I would know him anywhere. He turns back to me. "But you want to know more."

"Yes," I say. "I do."

"I'm here. Isn't that enough?"

I think about that for a minute. I suppose it is. I don't really want to know. What would I do with the details? I know enough, I know too much. I don't want the burden of all this knowledge. Is this what I came to Plover Island for? If I did, it was a mistake. I think about James, Denis, the house, the cats, the long road I have to travel.

I unwrap the gun from the plastic. It's exactly the same. Everything is the same.

"Why do you have the gun, Chrissie?"

We stare at each other. He knows why I have the gun, I don't have to tell him. I look at him in the darkening light, and quickly, quickly, I point the gun and pull the trigger.